# *an Englishwoman's*
# LOVE LETTERS

by Anonymous

Welcome Rain Publishers
New York

AN ENGLISHWOMAN'S LOVE LETTERS
by Anonymous

First Welcome Rain edition 2000
Printed in Canada.

First published in 1900 in England
by John Murray,
and in the United States
by Doubleday, Page & Co., New York.

Direct any inquiries to Welcome Rain Publishers LLC
225 West 35th Street, Suite 1100
New York, NY 10001

ISBN 1-56649-168-1
Manufactured in Canada by BLAZE I.P.I.

First Edition: September 2000
1  3  5  7  9  10  8  6  4  2

LAKE LUCERNE. P. 112.

# AN ENGLISHWOMAN'S LOVE-LETTERS.

## EXPLANATION.

It need hardly be said that the woman by whom these letter were written had no thought that they would be read by anyone but the person to whom they were addressed. But a request, conveyed under circumstances which the writer herself would have regarded as all-commanding, urges that they should now be given to the world; and, so far as is possible with a due regard to the claims of privacy, what is here printed presents the letters as they were first written in their complete form and sequence.

Very little has been omitted which in any way bears upon the devotion of which they are a record. A few names of persons and localities have been changed; and several short notes (not above twenty in all), together with some passages bearing too intimately upon events which might be recognized, have been left out without indication of their omission.

It was a necessary condition to the present publication that the authorship of these letters should remain unstated. Those who know will keep silence; those who do not, will not find here any data likely to guide them to the truth.

The story which darkens these pages cannot be more fully indicated while the feelings of some who are still living have to be consulted; nor will the reader find the root of the tragedy explained in the letters themselves. But one thing at least may be said as regards the principal actors—that to the memory of neither of them does any blame belong. They were equally the victims of circumstances, which came whole out of the hands of fate and remained, so far as one of the two was concerned, a mystery to the day of her death.

## LETTER I.

BELOVED: This is your first letter from me:
yet it is not the first I have written to you. There
are letters to you lying at love's dead-letter office
in this same writing—so many, my memory has
lost count of them!

This is my confession: I told you I had one
to make, and you laughed:—you did not know
how serious it was—for to be in love with you
long before you were in love with me—nothing
can be more serious than that!

You deny that I was: yet I know when you
first really loved me. All at once, one day
something about me came upon you as a surprise: and how, except on the road to love, can
there be surprises? And in the surprise came
love. You did not *know* me before. Before
then, it was only the other nine entanglements
which take hold of the male heart and occupy
it till the tenth is ready to make one knot of
them all.

In the letter written that day, I said, "You
love me." I could never have said it before;

though I had written twelve letters to my love
for you, I had not once been able to write of
your love for me.  Was not *that* serious?

Now I have confessed!  I thought to discover myself all blushes, but my face is cool: you
have kissed all my blushes away!  Can I ever
be ashamed in your eyes now, or grow rosy because of anything *you* or *I* think?  So!—you
have robbed me of one of my charms: I am
brazen.  Can you love me still?

You love me, you love me; you are wonderful! we are both wonderful, you and I.

Well, it is good for you to know I have waited
and wished, long before the thing came true.
But to see *you* waiting and wishing, when the
thing *was* true all the time:—oh! that was the
trial!  How not suddenly to throw my arms
round you and cry, " Look, see! O blind mouth,
why are you famished? "

And you never knew?  Dearest, I love you
for it, you never knew!  I believe a man, when
he finds he has won, thinks he has taken the city
by assault: he does not guess how to the in-
siders it has been a weary siege, with flags of surrender fluttering themselves to rags from every
wall and window!  No: in love it is the women
who are the strategists; and they have at last
to fall into the ambush they know of with a
good grace.

You must let me praise myself a little for the past, since I can never praise myself again. You must do that for me now! There is not a battle left for me to win. You and peace hold me so much a prisoner, have so caught me from my own way of living, that I seem to hear a pin drop twenty years ahead of me: it seems an event! Dearest, a thousand times, I would not have it be otherwise: I am only too willing to drop out of existence altogether and find myself in your arms instead. Giving you my love, I can so easily give you my life. Ah, my dear, I am yours so utterly, so gladly! Will you ever find it out, you who took so long to discover anything?

## LETTER II.

DEAREST: Your name woke me this morning: I found my lips piping their song before I was well back into my body out of dreams. I wonder if the rogues babble when my spirit is nesting? Last night you were a high tree and I was in it, the wind blowing us both; but I forget the rest,—whatever, it was enough to make me wake happy.

There are dreams that go out like candle-light directly one opens the shutters: they illumine the walls no longer; the daylight is too strong for them. So, now, I can hardly remember anything of my dreams: daylight, with you in it, floods them out.

Oh, how are you? Awake? Up? Have you breakfasted? I ask you a thousand things. You are thinking of me, I know: but what are you thinking? I am devoured by curiosity about myself—none at all about you, whom I have all by heart! If I might only know how happy I make you, and just *which* thing I said yesterday is making you laugh to-day—I could cry with joy over being the person I am.

It is you who make me think so much about myself, trying to find myself out. I used to be most self-possessed, and regarded it as the crowning virtue: and now—your possession of me sweeps it away, and I stand crying to be let into a secret that is no longer mine. Shall I ever know *why* you love me? It is my religious difficulty; but it never rises into a doubt. You *do* love me, I know. *Why*, I don't think I ever can know.

You ask me the same question about yourself, and it becomes absurd, because I altogether belong to you. If I hold my breath for a moment wickedly (for I can't do it breathing), and try to look at the world with you out of it, I seem to have fallen over a precipice; or rather, the solid earth has slipped from under my feet, and I am off into vacuum. Then, as I take breath again for fear, my star swims up and clasps me, and shows me your face. O happy star this that I was born under, that moved with me and winked quiet prophecies at me all through my childhood, I not knowing what it meant:—the dear radiant thing naming to me my lover!

As a child, now and then, and for no reason, I used to be sublimely happy: real wings took

hold of me. Sometimes a field became fairy-
land as I walked through it; or a tree poured out
a scent that its blossoms never had before or
after. I think now that those must have been
moments when you too were in like contact with
earth,—had your feet in grass which felt a faint
ripple of wind, or stood under a lilac in a
drench of fragrance that had grown double after
rain.

When I asked you about the places of your
youth, I had some fear of finding that we might
once have met, and that I had not remembered it
as the summing up of my happiness in being
young. Far off I see something undiscovered
waiting us, something I could not have guessed
at before—the happiness of being old. Will it
not be something like the evening before last
when we were sitting together, your hand in
mine, and one by one, as the twilight drew about
us, the stars came and took up their stations
overhead? They seemed to me then to be following out some quiet train of thought in the
universal mind: the heavens were remembering
the stars back into their places:—the Ancient of
Days drawing upon the infinite treasures of
memory in his great lifetime. Will not Love's
old age be the same to us both—a starry place
of memories?

Your dear letter is with me while I write: how

shortly you are able to say everything! To-morrow you will come. What more do I want —except to-morrow itself, with more promises of the same thing?

You are at my heart, dearest: nothing in the world can be nearer to me than you!

## LETTER III.

DEAREST AND RIGHTLY BELOVED: You cannot tell how your gift has pleased me; or rather you *can*, for it shows you have a long memory back to our first meeting: though at the time I was the one who thought most of it.

It is quite true; you have the most beautifully shaped memory in Christendom: these are the very books in the very edition I have long wanted, and have been too humble to afford myself. And now I cannot stop to read one, for joy of looking at them all in a row. I will kiss you for them all, and for more besides: indeed it is the " besides " which brings you my kisses at all.

Now that you have chosen so perfectly to my mind, I may proffer a request which, before, I was shy of making. It seems now beneficently anticipated. It is that you will not ever let your gifts take the form of jewelry, not after the ring which you are bringing me: *that*, you know, I both welcome and wish for. But, as to the rest, the world has supplied me with a feeling against jewelry as a love-symbol. Look abroad and you will see: it is too possessive, too much like " chains of office "—the fair one is to wear her radiant harness before the world, that other women may be envious and the desire of her master's eye be satisfied! Ah, no!

I am yours, dear, utterly; and nothing you give me would have that sense: I know you too well to think it. But in the face of the present fashion (and to flout it), which expects the lover to give in this sort, and the beloved to show herself a dazzling captive, let me cherish my ritual of opposition which would have no meaning if we were in a world of our own, and no place in my thoughts, dearest;—as it has not now, so far as you are concerned. But I am conscious I shall be looked at as your chosen; and I would choose my own way of how to look back most proudly.

And so for the books more thanks and more, —that they are what I would most wish, and not anything else: which, had they been, they would still have given me pleasure, since from you they could come only with a good meaning: and—diamonds even—I could have put up with them!

To-morrow you come for your ring, and bring me my own? Yours is here waiting. I have it on my finger, very loose, with another standing sentry over it to keep it from running away.

A mouse came out of my wainscot last night, and plunged me in horrible dilemma: for I am equally idiotic over the idea of the creature trapped or free, and I saw sleepless nights ahead of me till I had secured a change of locality for him.

To startle him back into hiding would have only deferred my getting truly rid of him, so I was most tiptoe and diplomatic in my doings. Finally, a paper bag, put into a likely nook with some sentimentally preserved wedding-cake crumbled into it, crackled to me of his arrival. In a brave moment I noosed the little beast, bag and all, and lowered him from the window by string, till the shrubs took from me the burden of responsibility.

I visited the bag this morning: he had eaten his way out, crumbs and all: and has, I suppose, become a fieldmouse, for the hay smells invitingly, and it is only a short run over the lawn and a jump over the ha-ha to be in it. Poor morsels, I prefer them so much undomesticated!

Now this mouse is no allegory, and the paper bag is *not* a diamond necklace, in spite of the wedding-cake sprinkled over it! So don't say that this letter is too hard for your understanding, or you will frighten me from telling you anything foolish again. Brains are like jewels in this, difference of surface has nothing to do with the size and value of them. Yours is a beautiful smooth round, like a pearl, and mine all facets and flashes like cut glass. And yours so much the bigger, and I love it so much the best! The trap which caught me was baited with one great pearl. So the mouse comes in with a meaning tied to its tail after all!

## LETTER  IV.

In all the world, dearest, what is more unequal
than love between a man and a woman?  I have
been spending an amorous morning and want to
share it with you: but lo, the task of bringing
that bit of my life into your vision is altogether
beyond me.

What have I been doing?  Dear man, I have
been dressmaking! and dress, when one is in the
toils, is but a love-letter writ large.  You will
see and admire the finished thing, but you will
take no interest in the composition.  Therefore
I say your love is unequal to mine.

For think how ravished I would be if you
brought me a coat and told me it was all your
own making!  One day you had thrown down
a mere tailor-made thing in the hall, and yet I
kissed it as I went by.  And that was at a time
when we were only at the handshaking stage, the
palsied beginnings of love:—*you*, I mean!

But oh, to get you interested in the dress I
was making to you to-day!—the beautiful flowing opening,—not too flowing: the elaborate cen-

tral composition where the heart of me has to come, and the wind-up of the skirt, a long reluctant tailing-off, full of commas and colons of ribbon to make it seem longer, and insertions everywhere. I dreamed myself in it, retiring through the door after having bidden you good-night, and you watching the long disappearing eloquence of that tail, still saying to you as it vanished, " Good-by, good-by. I love you so! see me, how slowly I am going!"

Well, that is a bit of my dress-making, a very corporate part of my affection for you; and you are not a bit interested, for I have shown you none of the seamy side; it is that which interests you male creatures, Zolaites, every one of you.

And what have you to show similar, of the thought of me entering into all your masculine pursuits? Do you go out rabbit-shooting for the love of me? If so, I trust you make a miss of it every time! That you are a sportsman is one of the very hardest things in life that I have to bear.

Last night Peterkins came up with me to keep guard against any further intrusion of mice. I put her to sleep on the couch: but she discarded the red shawl I had prepared for her at the bottom, and lay at the top most uncomfortably in a parcel of millinery into which from one end I had already made excavations, so that it formed a large bag. Into the further end of this bag Turks crept and snuggled down: but every time she turned in the night (and it seemed very often) the brown paper crackled and woke me up. So at last I took it up and shook out its contents; and Pippins slept soundly on red flannel till Nan-nan brought the tea.

You will notice that in this small narrative Peterkins gets three names: it is a fashion that runs through the household, beginning with the Mother-Aunt, who on some days speaks of Nan-nan as "the old lady," and sometimes as "that girl," all according to the two tempers she has about Nan-nan's privileged position in regard to me.

You were only here yesterday, and already I want you again so much, so much!

Your never satisfied but always loving.

## LETTER V.

Most Beloved: I have been thinking, staring at this blank piece of paper, and wondering how *there* am I ever to say what I have in me here—not wishing to say anything at all, but just to be! I feel that I am living now only because you love me: and that my life will have run out, like this penful of ink, when that use in me is past. Not yet, Beloved, oh, not yet! Nothing is finished that we have to do and be:— hardly begun! I will not call even this " midsummer," however much it seems so: it is still only spring.

Every day your love binds me more deeply than I knew the day before: so that no day is the same now, but each one a little happier than the last. My own, you are my very own! And yet, true as that is, it is not so true as that I am *your* own. It is less absolute, I mean; and must be so, because I cannot very well *take* possession of anything when I am given over heart and soul out of my own possession: there isn't enough identity left in me, I am yours so much, so much!

All this is useless to say, yet what can I say else, if I have to begin saying anything?

Could I truly be your " star and goddess," as you call me, Beloved, I would do you the service of Thetis at least (who did it for a greater than herself)—

> " Bid Heaven and Earth combine their charms,
>     And round you early, round you late,
>   Briareus fold his hundred arms
>     To guard you from your single fate."

But I haven't got power over an eight-armed octopus even: so am merely a very helpless loving nonentity which merges itself most happily in you, and begs to be lifted to no pedestal at all, at all.

If you love me in a manner that is at all possible, you will see that " goddess " does not suit me. " Star " I would I were now, with a wide eye to carry my looks to you over this horizon which keeps you invisible. Choose one, if you will, dearest, and call it mine: and to me it shall be yours: so that when we are apart and the stars come out, our eyes may meet up at the same point in the heavens, and be " keeping company " for us among the celestial bodies—with their permission: for I have too lively a sense of their beauty not to be a little superstitious about them. Have you not felt for yourself a sort of physiog-

nomy in the constellations,—most of them seeming benevolent and full of kind regards:—but
not all? I am always glad when the Great Bear
goes away from my window, fine beast though
he is: he seems to growl at me! No doubt it is
largely a question of names; and what's in a
name? In yours, Beloved, when I speak it, more
than I can compass!

## LETTER VI.

BELOVED: I have been trusting to fate, while keeping silence, that something from you was to come to-day and make me specially happy. And it has: bless you abundantly! You have undone and got round all I said about "jewelry," though this is nothing of the sort, but a shrine: so my word remains. I have it with me now, safe hidden, only now and then it comes out to have a look at me,—smiles and goes back again. Dearest, you must *feel* how I thank you, for I cannot say it: body and soul I grow too much blessed with all that you have given me, both visibly and invisibly, and always perfectly.

And as for the day: I have been thinking you the most uncurious of men, because you had not asked: and supposed it was too early days yet for you to remember that I had ever been born. To-day is my birthday! you said nothing, so I said nothing; and yet this has come: I trusted my star to show its sweet influences in its own way. Or, after all, did you know, and had you asked anyone but me? Yet had you known, you would have wished me the "happy returns" which among all your dear words to me you do not. So I take it that the motion comes straight to you from heaven; and, in the event, you will pardon me for having been still secretive and shy in not telling what you did not inquire after. *Yours*, I knew, dear, quite long ago, so had no need to ask you for it. And it is six months before you will be in the same year with me again, and give to twenty-two all the companionable sweetness that twenty-one has been having.

Many happy returns of *my* birthday to you, dearest! That is all that my birthdays are for. Have you been happy to-day, I wonder? and am wondering also whether this evening we shall see you walking quietly in and making everything into perfection that has been trembling just on the verge of it all day long.

One drawback of my feast is that I have to write short to you; for there are other correspondents who on this occasion look for quick answers, and not all of them to be answered in an offhand way. Except you, it is the coziest whom I keep waiting; but elders have a way with them—even kind ones: and when they condescend to write upon an anniversary, we have to skip to attention or be in their bad books at once.

So with the sun still a long way out of bed,

I have to tuck up these sheets for you, as if the good of the day had already been sufficient unto itself and its full tale had been told. Good-night. It is so hard to take my hands off writing to you, and worry on at the same exercise in another direction. I kiss you more times than I can count: it is almost really you that I kiss now! My very dearest, my own sweetheart, whom I so worship. Good-night! "Good-afternoon" sounds too funny: is outside our vocabulary altogether. While I live, I must love you more than I know!

## LETTER VII.

My Friend: Do you think this a cold way of beginning? I do not: is it not the true send-off of love? I do not know how men fall in love: but I could not have had that come-down in your direction without being your friend first. Oh, my dear, and after, after; it is but a limitless friendship I have grown into!

I have heard men run down the friendships of women as having little true substance. Those who speak so, I think, have never come across a real case of woman's friendship. I praise my own sex, dearest, for I know some of their loneliness, which you do not: and until a certain date their friendship was the deepest thing in life I had met with.

For must it not be true that a woman becomes more absorbed in friendship than a man, since friendship may have to mean so much more to her, and cover so far more of her life, than it does to the average man? However big a man's capacity for friendship, the beauty of it does not fill his whole horizon for the future: he still looks ahead of it for the mate who will complete his life, giving his body and soul the complement they require. Friendship alone does not satisfy him: he makes a bigger claim on life, regarding certain possessions as his right.

But a woman:—oh, it is a fashion to say the best women are sure to find husbands, and have, if they care for it, the certainty before them of a full life. I know it is not so. There are women, wonderful ones, who come to know quite early in life that no men will ever wish to make wives of them: for them, then, love in friendship is all that remains, and the strongest wish of all that can pass through their souls with hope for its fulfillment is to be a friend to somebody.

It is man's arrogant certainty of his future which makes him impatient of the word "friendship": it cools life to his lips, he so confident that the headier nectar is his due!

I came upon a little phrase the other day that touched me so deeply: it said so well what I have wanted to say since we have known each other. Some peasant rhymer, an Irishman, is singing his love's praises, and sinks his voice from the height of his passionate superlatives to call her his "share of the world." Peasant and Irishman, he knew that his fortune did not embrace the universe: but for him his love was just that—his share of the world.

Surely when in anyone's friendship we seem

to have gained our share of the world, that is all that can be said. It means all that we can take in, the whole armful the heart and senses are capable of, or that fate can bestow. And for how many that must be friendship—especially for how many women!

My dear, you are my share of the world, also my share of Heaven: but there I begin to speak of what I do not know, as is the way with happy humanity. All that my eyes could dream of waking or sleeping, all that my ears could be most glad to hear, all that my heart could beat faster to get hold of—your friendship gave me suddenly as a bolt from the blue.

My friend, my friend, my friend! If you could change or go out of my life now, the sun would drop out of my heavens: I should see the world with a great piece gashed out of its side,—my share of it gone. No, I should not see it, I don't think I should see anything ever again,—not truly.

Is it not strange how often to test our happiness we harp on sorrow? I do: don't let it weary you. I know I have read somewhere that great love always entails pain. I have not found it yet: but, for me, it does mean fear,—the sort of fear I had as a child going into big buildings. I loved them: but I feared, because of their big-ness, they were likely to tumble on me.

But when I begin to think you may be too big for me, I remember you as my "friend," and the fear goes for a time, or becomes that sort of fear I would not part with if I might.

I have no news for you: only the old things to tell you, the wonder of which ever remains new. How holy your face has become to me: as I saw it last, with something more than the usual proofs of love for me upon it—a look as if your love troubled you!  I know the trouble: I feel it, dearest, in my own woman's way.  Have patience.—When I see you so, I feel that prayer is the only way given me for saying what my love for you wishes to be.  And yet I hardly ever pray in words.

Dearest, be happy when you get this: and, when you can, come and give my happiness its rest.  Till then it is a watchman on the lookout.

" Night-night!"  Your true sleepy one.

## LETTER VIII.

Now *why*, I want to know, Beloved, was I so specially " good " to you in my last? I have been quite as good to you fifty times before,— if such a thing can be from me to you. Or do you mean good *for* you? Then, dear, I must be sorry that the thing stands out so much as an exception!

Oh, dearest Beloved, for a little I think I must not love you so much, or must not let you see it.

When does your mother return, and when am I to see her? I long to so much. Has she still not written to you about our news?

I woke last night to the sound of a great flock of sheep going past. I suppose they were going by forced marches to the fair over at Hylesbury. It was in the small hours: and a few of them lifted up their voices and complained of this robbery of night and sleep in the night. They were so tired, so tired, they said: and so did the muffawully patter of their poor feet. The lambs said most; and the sheep agreed with a husky croak.

I said a prayer for them, and went to sleep
again as the sound of the lambs died away; but
somehow they stick in my heart, those sad sheep
driven along through the night.    It was in its
degree like the woman hurrying along, who said,
" My God, my God!" that summer Sunday
morning.    These notes from lives that appear
and disappear remain endlessly; and I do not
think our hearts can have been made so sensitive
to suffering we can do nothing to relieve, without some good reason.    So I tell you this, as I
would any sorrow of my own, because it has become a part of me, and is underlying all that I
think to-day.

I am to expect you the day after to-morrow,
but " not for certain "?    Thus you give and you
take away, equally blessed in either case.    All
the same, I shall *certainly* expect you, and be disappointed if on Thursday at about this hour
your way be not my way.

" How shall I my true love know " if he does
not come often enough to see me?    Sunshine be
on you all possible hours till we meet again.

## LETTER IX.

BELOVED: Is the morning looking at you as it is looking at me? A little to the right of the sun there lies a small cloud, filmy and faint, but enough to cast a shadow somewhere. From this window, high up over the view, I cannot see where the shadow of it falls,—further than my eye can reach: perhaps just now over you, since you lie further west. But I cannot be sure. We cannot be sure about the near things in this world; only about what is far off and fixed.

You and I looking up see the same sun, if there are no clouds over us: but we may not be looking at the same clouds even when both our hearts are in shadow. That is so, even when hearts are as close together as yours and mine: they respond to the same light: but each one has its own roof of shadow, wearing its rue with a world of difference.

Why is it? why can no two of us have sorrows quite in common? What can be nearer together than our wills to be one? In joy we are; and yet, though I reach and reach, and sadden if you are sad, I cannot make your sorrow my own.

I suppose sorrow is of the earth earthy: and all that is of earth makes division. Every joy that belongs to the body casts shadows somewhere. I wonder if there can enter into us a joy that has no shadow anywhere? The joy of having you has behind it the shadow of parting; is there any way of loving that would make parting no sorrow at all? To me, now, the idea seems treason! I cling to my sorrow that you are not here: I send up my cloud, as it were, to catch the sun's brightness: it is a kite that I pull with my heart-strings.

To the sun of love the clouds that cover absence must look like white flowers in the green fields of earth, or like doves hovering: and he reaches down and strokes them with his warm beams, making all their feathers like gold.

Some clouds let the gold come through; *mine*, now.—That cloud I saw away to the right is coming this way toward me. I can see the shadow of it now, moving along a far-off strip of road: and I wonder if it is *your* cloud, with you under it coming to see me again!

When you come, why am I any happier than when I know you are coming? It is the same thing in love. I have you now all in my mind's eye; I have you by heart; have I my arms a bit more round you then than now?

How it puzzles me that, when love is perfect,

there should be disappearances and reappear-
ances: and faces now and then showing a
change!—You, actually, the last time you came,
looking a day older than the day before! What
was it? Had old age blown you a kiss, or given
you a wrinkle in the art of dying? Or had you
turned over some new leaf, and found it withered on the other side?

I could not see how it was: I heard you coming—it was spring! The door opened:—oh, it
was autumnal! One day had fallen away like
a leaf out of my forest, and I had not been there
to see it go!

At what hour of the twenty-four does a day
shed itself out of our lives? Not, I think, on the
stroke of the clock, at midnight, or at cock-crow.
Some people, perhaps, would say—with the first
sleep; and that the " beauty-sleep " is the new
day putting out its green wings. *I* think it must
be not till something happens to make the new
day a stronger impression than the last. So it
would please me to think that your yesterday
dropped off as you opened the door; and that,
had I peeped and seen you coming up the stairs,
I should have seen you looking a day younger.

*That* means that you age at the sight of me!
I think you do. I, I feel a hundred on the road
to immortality, directly your face dawns on me.

There's a foot gone over my grave! The

angel of the resurrection with his mouth pursed fast to his trumpet!—Nothing else than the gallop-a-gallop of your horse:—it sounds like a kettle boiling over!

So this goes into hiding: listens to us all the while we talk; and comes out afterwards with all its blushes stale, to be rouged up again and sent off the moment your back is turned.  No, better!—to be slipped into your pocket and carried home to yourself *by* yourself.  How, when you get to your destination and find it, you will curse yourself that you were not a speedier postman!

## LETTER X.

DEAREST: Did you find your letter? The quicker I post, the quicker I need to sit down and write again. The grass under love's feet never stops growing: I must make hay of it while the sun shines.

You say my metaphors make you giddy.—My dear, you, without a metaphor in your composition, do that to me! So it is not for you to complain; your curses simply fly back to roost. Where do you pigeon-hole them? In a pie? (I mean to write now until I have made you as giddy as a dancing dervish!) *Your* letters are much more like blackbirds: and I have a pie of them here, twenty-four at least; and when I open it they sing "Chewee, chewee, chewee!" in the most scared way!

Your last but three said most solemnly, just as if you meant it, "I hope you don't keep these miserables! Though I fill up my hollow hours with them, there is no reason why they should fill up yours." You added that I was better oc-

cupied—and here I am " better occupied " even as
you bid me.

But one can jump best from a spring-board:
and how could I jump as far as your arms by letter, if I had not yours to jump from?

So you see they are kept, and my disobedience
of you has begun: and I find disobedience wonderfully sweet.  But then, you gave me a law
which you knew I should disobey:—that is the
way the world began.  It is not for nothing that
I am a daughter of Eve.

And here is our world in our hands, yours and
mine, now in the making.  Which day are the
evening and the morning now?  I think it must
be the birds'—and already, with the wings, disobedience has been reached!  Make much of it!
the day will come when I shall wish to obey.
There are moments when I feel a wish taking
hold of me stronger than I can understand, that
you should command me beyond myself—to
things I have not strength or courage for of my
own accord.  How close, dearest, when that day
comes, my heart will feel itself to yours!  It feels
close now: but it is to your feet I am nearest, as
yet.  Lift me!  There, there, Beloved, I kiss you
with all my will.  Oh, dear heart, forgive me for
being no more than I am: your freehold to all
eternity!

## LETTER XI.

Oh, Dearest: I have danced and I have danced till I am tired! I am dropping with sleep, but I must just touch you and say good-night. This was our great day of publishing, dearest, *ours:* all the world knows it; and all admire your choice! I was determined they should. I have been collecting scalps for you to hang at your girdle. All thought me beautiful: people who never did so before. I wanted to say to them, " Am I not beautiful? I am, am I not? " And it was not for myself I was asking this praise. Beloved, I was wearing the magic rose—what you gave me when we parted: you saying, alas, that you were not to be there. But you *were!* Its leaves have not dropped nor the scent of it faded. I kiss you out of the heart of it. Good-night: come to me in my first dream!

## LETTER XII.

DEAREST: It has been such a funny day from post-time onwards:—congratulations on the great event are beginning to arrive in envelopes and on wheels. Some are very kind and dear; and some are not so—only the ordinary seemliness of polite sniffle-snaffle. Just after you had gone yesterday, Mrs. —— called and was told the news. Of course she knew *of* you: but didn't think she had ever seen you. "Probably he passed you at the gates," I said. "What?" she went off with a view-hallo; "that well-dressed sort of young fellow in gray, and a mustache, and knowing how to ride? Met us in the lane. *Well,* my dear, I *do* congratulate you!"

And whether it was by the gray suit, or the mustache, or the knowing how to ride that her congratulations were so emphatically secured, I know not!

Others are yet more quaint, and more to my liking. Nan-nan is Nan-nan: I cannot let you off what she said! No tears or sentiment came from her to prevent me laughing: she brisked like an old war-horse at the first word of it, and blessed God that it had come betimes, that she might be a nurse again in her old age! She is a true " Mrs. Berry," and is ready to make room for you in my affections for the sake of far-off divine events, which promise renewed youth to her old bones.

Roberts, when he brought me my pony this morning, touched his hat quick twice over to show that the news brimmed in his body: and a very nice cordial way of showing, I thought it! He was quite ready to talk when I let him go; and he gave me plenty of good fun. He used to know you when he was in service at the H——s, and speaks of you as being then " a gallous young hound," whatever that may mean. I imagine " gallous " to be a rustic Lewis Carroll compound, made up in equal parts of callousness and gallantry, which most boys are, at some stage of their existence.

What tales will you be getting of me out of Nan-nan, some day behind my back, I wonder? There is one I shall forbid her to reveal: it shall be part of my marriage-portion to show you early that you have got a wife with a temper!

Here is a whole letter that must end now,— and the great Word never mentioned! It is good for you to be put upon *maigre* fare, for once. I

hol*d* my pen back with b*o*th hands: it wants so
much to gi*v*e you the forbidd*e*n treat.  Oh, the
serpent in the garden!  See where it has un-
derlined its meaning.  Frailty, thy pen is a J
pen!

Adieu, adieu, remember me.

## LETTER XIII.

The letters? No, Beloved, I could not! Not yet. There you have caught me where I own I am still shy of you.

A long time hence, when we are a safely wedded pair, you shall turn them over. It *may* be a short time; but I will keep them however long. Indeed I must ever keep them; they talk to me of the dawn of my existence,—the early light before our sun rose, when my love of you was growing and had not yet reached its full.

If I disappoint you I will try to make up for it with something I wrote long before I ever saw you. To-day I was turning over old things my mother had treasured for me of my childhood— of days spent with her: things of laughter as well as of tears; such a dear selection, so quaint and sweet, with moods of her as I dimly remember her to have been. And among them was this absurdity, written, and I suppose placed in the mouth of my stocking, the Christmas I stayed with her in France. I remember the time as a great treat, but nothing of this. " Nilgoes " is " Nicholas," you must understand! How he must have laughed over me asleep while he read this!

"Cher père Nilgoes. S'il vous plait voulez vous me donné plus de jeux que des oranges des pommes et des pombons parc que nous allons faire l'arbre de noel cette anné et les jeaux ferait mieux pour l'arbre de Noel. Il ne faut pas dire à petite mere s'il vous plait parce que je ne veut pas quelle sache sil vous voulez venir ce soir du ceil pour que vous pouvez me donner ce que je vous demande Dites bon jour à la St. Viearge est á l'enfant Jeuses et à Ste Joseph. Adieu cher St. Nilgoes."

I haven't altered the spelling, I love it too well, prophetic of a fault I still carry about me. How strange that little bit of invocation to the dear folk above sounds to me now! My mother must have been teaching me things after her own persuasion; most naturally, poor dear one—though that too has gone like water off my mind. It was one of the troubles between her and my father: the compact that I was to be brought up a Catholic was dissolved after they separated; and I am sorry, thinking it unjust to her; yet glad, content with being what I am.

I must have been less than five when I penned this: I was always a letter-writer, it seems.

It is a reproach now from many that I have ceased to be: and to them I fear it is true. That I have not truly ceased, " witness under my hand these presents,"—or whatever may be the proper legal terms for an affidavit.

What were *you* like, Beloved, as a very small child? Should I have loved you from the beginning had we toddled to the rencounter; and would my love have passed safely through the " gallous young hound " period; and could I love you more now in any case, had I *all* your days treasured up in my heart, instead of less than a year of them?

How strangely much have seven miles kept our fates apart! It seems uncharacteristic for this small world,—where meetings come about so far above the dreams of average—to have played us such a prank.

This must do for this once, Beloved; for behold me busy to-day: with *what,* I shall not tell you. I would like to put you to a test, as ladies did their knights of old, and hardly ever do now—fearing, I suppose, lest the species should altogether fail them at the pinch. I would like to see if you could come here and sit with me from beginning to end, *with your eyes shut:* never once opening them. I am not saying whether I think curiosity, or affection, would make the attempt too difficult. But if you were sure you could, you might come here to-morrow—a day otherwise interdicted. Only know, having come, that if you open those dear cupboards of vision and set eyes on things not yet intended to be looked at, there will be confusion of tongues in this Tower we are building whose top is to reach heaven. Will you come? I don't *say* " come "; I only want to know—will you?

To-day my love flies low over the earth like a swallow before rain, and touching the tops of the flowers has culled you these. Kiss them until they open: they are full of my thoughts, as the world, to me, is full of you,

## LETTER XIV.

OWN DEAREST : Come I did not think that you
would, or mean that you should seriously; for is
it not a poor way of love to make the object of it
cut an absurd or partly absurd figure? I wrote
only as a woman having a secret on the tip of her
tongue and the tips of her fingers, and full of a
longing to say it and send it.

Here it is at last: love me for it, I have worked
so hard to get it done! And you do not know
why and what for? Beloved, it—*this*—is the
anniversary of the day we first met; and you have
forgotten it already or never remembered it:—
and yet have been clamoring for " the letters "!

On the first anniversary of our marriage, *if
you remember it,* you shall have those same letters : and not otherwise. So there they lie safe
till doomsday!

The M.-A. has been very gracious and dear
after her little outbreak of yesterday : her repent-
ances, after I have hurt her feelings, are so gen-
tle and sweet, they always fill me with compunc-
tion. Finding that I would go on with the thing
I was doing, she volunteered to come and read
to me: a requiem over the bone of contention
which we had gnawed between us. Was not

that pretty and charitable? She read Tennyson's Life for a solid hour, and continued it today. Isn't it funny that she should take up such a book?—she who "can't abide" Tennyson or Browning or Shakespeare: only likes Byron, I suppose because it was the right and fashionable liking when she was young. Yet she is plodding through the Life religiously—only skipping the verses. I have come across two little specimens of "Death and the child" in it. His son, Lionel, was carried out in a blanket one night in the great comet year, and waking up under the stars asked, "Am I dead?" Number two is of a little girl at Wellington's funeral who saw his charger carrying his *boots,* and asked, "Shall I be like that after I die?"

A queer old lady came to lunch yesterday, a great traveler, though lame on two crutches. We carefully hid all guide-books and maps, and held our peace about next month, lest she should insist on coming too: though I think Nineveh was the place she was most anxious to go to, if the M.-A. would consent to accompany her!

Good-by, dearest of one-year-old acquaintances! you, too, send your blessing on the anniversary, now that my better memory has reminded you of it! All that follow we will bless in company. I trust you are one-half as happy as I am, my own, my own.

## LETTER XV.

You told me, dearest, that I should find your mother formidable. It is true; I did. She is a person very much in the grand pagan style: I admire it, but I cannot flow in that sort of company, and I think she meant to crush me. You were very wise to leave her to come alone.

I like her: I mean I believe that under that terribleness she has a heart of gold, which once opened would never shut: but she has not opened it to me. I believe she could have a great charity, that no evil-doing would dismay her: " stanch " sums her up. But I have done nothing wrong enough yet to bring me into her good graces. Loving her son, even, though, I fear, a great offense, has done me no good turn.

Perhaps that is her inconsistency: women are sure to be inconsistent somewhere: it is their birthright.

I began to study her at once, to find *you:* it did not take long. How I could love her, if she would let me!

You know her far far better than I, and want

no advice: otherwise I would say—never praise me to her; quote my follies rather! To give ground for her distaste to revel in will not deepen me in her bad books so much as attempts to warp her judgment.

I need not go through it all: she will have told you all that is to the purpose about our meeting. She bristled in, a brave old fighting figure, announcing compulsion in every line, but with all her colors flying. She waited for the door to close, then said, " My son has bidden me come, I suppose it is my duty: he is his own master now."

We only shook hands. Our talk was very little of you. I showed her all the horses, the dogs, and the poultry; she let the inspection appear to conclude with myself: asked me my habits, and said I looked healthy. I owned I felt it. " Looks and feelings are the most deceptive things in the world," she told me; adding that " poor stock " got more than its share of these. And when she said it I saw quite plainly that she meant me.

I wonder where she gets the notion: for we are a long-lived race, both sides of the family. I guessed that she would like frankness, and was as frank as I could be, pretending no deference to her objections. " You think you suit each other?" she asked me. My answer, " He suits me!" pleased her maternal palate, I think. "Any girl might say that!" she admitted. (She might indeed!)

This is the part of our interview she will not have repeated to you.

I was due at Hillyn when she was preparing to go: Aunt N—— came in, and I left her to do the honors while I slipped on my habit. I rode by your mother's carriage as far as the Greenway, where we branched. I suppose that is what her phrase means that you quote about my "making a trophy of her," and marching her a prisoner across the borders before all the world!

I do like her: she is worth winning. Can one say warmer of a future mother-in-law who stands hostile?

All the same it was an ordeal. I believe I have wept since: for Benjy scratched my door often yesterday evening, and looked most wistful when I came out. Merely paltry self-love, dearest:—I am so little accustomed to not being—liked.

I think she will be more gracious in her own house. I have her formal word that I am to come. Soon, not too soon, I will come over; and you shall meet me and take me to see her. There is something in her opposition that I can't fathom: I wondered twice was lunacy her notion: she looked at me so hard.

My mother's seclusion and living apart from

us was not on *that* account.   I often saw her: she was very dear and sweet to me, and had quiet eyes the very reverse of a person mentally deranged.   My father, I know, went to visit her when she lay dying; and I remember we all wore mourning.   My uncle has told me they had a deep regard for each other: but disagreed, and were independent enough to choose living apart.

I do not remember my father ever speaking of her to us as children: but I am sure there was no state of health to be concealed.

Last night I was talking to Aunt N—— about her.   "A very dear woman," she told me, "but your father was never so much alive to her worth as the rest of us."   Of him she said, "A dear, fine fellow: but not at all easy to get on with."   Him, of course, I have a continuous recollection of, and "a fine fellow" we did think him.   My mother comes to me more rarely, at intervals.

Don't talk me down your mother's throat: but tell her as much as she cares to know of this.   I am very proud of my "stock" which she thinks "poor"!

Dear, how much I have written on things which can never concern us finally, and so should not ruffle us while they last!   Hold me in your heart always, always; and the world may turn adamant to me for aught I care!   Be in my dreams tonight!

## LETTER XVI.

But, Dearest: When I think of you I never question whether what I think would be true or false in the eyes of others. All that concerns you seems to go on a different plane where evidence has no meaning or existence: where nobody exists or means anything, but only we two alone, engaged in bringing about for ourselves the still greater solitude of two into one. Oh, Beloved, what a company that will be! Take me in your arms, fasten me to your heart, breathe on me. Deny me either breath or the light of day: I am yours equally, to live or die at your word. I shut my eyes to feel your kisses falling on me like rain, or still more like sunshine,—yet most of all like kisses, my own dearest and best beloved!

Oh, we two! how wonderful we seem! And to think that there have been lovers like us since the world began: and the world not able to tell us one little word of it:—not well, so as to be believed—or only along with sadness where Fate has broken up the heavens which lay over some

pair of lovers.   Œnone's cry, " Ah me, my mountain shepherd," tells us of the joy when it has vanished, and most of all I get it in that song of wife
and husband which ends :—

> " Not a word for you,
>      Not a lock or kiss,
>           Good-by.
>   We, one, must part in two ;
>      Verily death is this :
>        I must die."

It was a woman wrote that : and we get love
there !   Is it only when joy is past that we can
give it its full expression ?   Even now, Beloved,
I break down in trying to say how I love you.   I
cannot put all my joy into my words, nor all my
love into my lips, nor all my life into your arms,
whatever way I try.   Something remains that I
cannot express.   Believe, dearest, that the half
has not yet been spoken, neither of my love for
you, nor of my trust in you,—nor of a wish that
seems sad, but comes in a very tumult of happiness—the wish to die so that some unknown good
may come to you out of me.

Not till you die, dearest, shall I die truly !   I
love you now too much for your heart not to
carry me to its grave, though I should die now,
and you live to be a hundred.   I pray you may !
I cannot choosè a day for you to die.   I am too

grateful to life which has given me to you to
say—if I were dying—"Come with me, dearest!" Though, how the words tempt me as I
write them!—Come with me, dearest: yes, come!
Ah, but you kiss me more, I think, when we say
good-by than when meeting; so you will kiss me
most of all when I have to die:—a thing in death
to look forward to! And, till then,—life, life,
till I am out of my depth in happiness and drown
in your arms!

Beloved, that I can write so to you,—think
what it means; what you have made me come
through in the way of love, that this, which I
could not have dreamed before, comes from me
with the thought of you! You told me to be
still—to let you "worship": I was to write back
acceptance of all your dear words. Are you
never to be at my feet, you ask. Indeed, dearest,
I do not know how, for I cannot move from
where I am! Do you feel where my thoughts
kiss you? You would be vexed with me if I
wrote it down, so I do not. And after all, some
day, under a bright star of Providence, I may
have gifts for you after my own mind which will
allow me to grow proud. Only now all the giving comes from you. It is I who am enriched
by your love, beyond knowledge of my former
self. Are *you* changed, dearest, by anything I
have done?

My heart goes to you like a tree in the wind, and all these thoughts are loose leaves that fly after you when I have to remain behind. Dear lover, what short visits yours seem! and the Mother-Aunt tells me they are most unconscionably long.—You will not pay any attention to *that,* please: forever let the heavens fall rather than that a hint to such foul effect should grow operative through me!

This brings you me so far as it can:—such little words off so great a body of—" liking " shall I call it? My paper stops me: it is my last sheet: I should have to go down to the library to get more—else I think I could not cease writing.

More love than I can name.—Ever, dearest, your own.

## LETTER XVII.

DEAREST: Do I not write you long letters? It reveals my weakness. I have thought (it had been coming on me, and now and then had broken out of me before I met you) that, left to myself, I should have become a writer of books—I scarcely can guess what sort—and gone contentedly into middle-age with that instead of *this* as my *raison d'être.*

How gladly I lay down that part of myself, and say—" But for you, I had been this quite other person, whom I have no wish to be now "! Beloved, your heart is the shelf where I put all my uncut volumes, wondering a little what sort of a writer I should have made; and chiefly wondering, would *you* have liked me in that character?

There is one here in the family who considers me a writer of the darkest dye, and does not approve of it. Benjy comes and sits most mournfully facing me when I settle down on a sunny morning, such as this, to write: and inquires, with all the dumbness a dog is capable of—" What has come between us, that you fill up your time and mine with those cat's-claw scratchings, when you should be in your wood-land dress running [with] me through damp places?"

Having written this sentimental meaning into his eyes, and Benjy still sitting watching me, I was seized with ruth for my neglect of him, and took him to see his mother's grave. At the bottom of the long walk is our dog's cemetery:—no tombstones, but mounds; and a dog-rose grows there and flourishes as nowhere else. It was my fancy as a child to have it planted: and I declare to you, it has taken wonderfully to the notion, as if it *knew* that it had relations of a higher species under its keeping. Benjy, too, has a profound air of knowing, and never scratches for bones there, as he does in other places. What horror, were I to find him digging up his mother's skeleton! Would my esteem for him survive?

When we got there to-day, he deprecated my choice of locality, asking what I had brought him *there* for. I pointed out to him the precise mound which covered the object of his earliest affections, and gathered you these buds. Are they not a deep color for wild ones?—if their blush remains a fixed state till the post brings them to you.

Through what flower would you best like to be passed back, as regards your material atoms, into

the spiritualized side of nature, when we have
done with ourselves in this life? No single
flower quite covers all my wants and aspirations.
You and I would put our heads together under-
ground and evolve a new flower—" carnation,
lily, lily, rose "—and send it up one fine morning
for scientists to dispute over and give diabolical
learned names to. What an end to our cozy
floral collaboration that would be!

Here endeth the epistle: the elect salutes you.
This week, if the authorities permit, I shall be
paying you a flying visit, with wings full of eyes,
—*and,* I hope, healing; for I believe you are
seedy, and that *that* is what is behind it. You
notice I have not complained. Dearest, how
could I! My happiness reaches to the clouds—
that is, to where things are not quite clear at
present. I love you no more than I ought: yet
far more than I can name. Good-night and
good-morning.—Your star, since you call me so.

## LETTER XVIII.

DEAREST: Not having had a letter from you this morning, I have read over some back ones, and find in one a bidding which I have never fulfilled, to tell you what I *do* all day. Was that to avoid the too great length of my telling you what I *think?* Yet you get more of me this way than that. What I do is every day so much the same: while what I think is always different. However, since you want a woman of action rather than of brain, here I start telling you.

I wake punctual and hungry at the sound of Nan-nan's drawing of the blinds: wait till she is gone (the old darling potters and tattles: it is her most possessive moment of me in the day, except when I sham headaches, and let her put me to bed) ; then I have my hand under my pillow and draw out your last for a reading that has lost count whether it is the twenty-second or the fifty-second time ;—discover new beauties in it, and run to the glass to discover new beauties in myself,—find them; Benjy comes up with the post's latest, and behold, my day is begun!

Is that the sort of thing you want to know? My days are without an action worth naming: I only think swelling thoughts, and write some of them: if ever I do anything worth telling, be sure I run a pen-and-ink race to tell you. No, it is man who *does* things; a woman only diddles (to adapt a word of diminutive sound for the occasion), unless, good, fortunate, independent thing, she works for her own living: and that is not me!

I feel sometimes as if a real bar were between me and a whole conception of life; because I have carpets and curtains, and Nan-nan, and Benjy, and last of all you—shutting me out from the realities of existence.

If you would all leave me just for one full moon, and come back to me only when I am starving for you all—for my tea to be brought to me in the morning, and all the paddings and cushionings which bolster me up from morning till night—with what a sigh of wisdom I would drop back into your arms, and would let you draw the rose-colored curtains round me again!

Now I am afraid lest I have become too happy: I am leaning so far out of window to welcome the dawn, I seem to be tempting a fall—heaven itself to fall upon me.

What do I *know* truly, who only know so much happiness?

Dearest, if there is anything else in love which I do not know, teach it me quickly: I am utterly yours. If there is sorrow to give, give it me! Only let me have with it the consciousness of your love.

Oh, my dear, I lose myself if I think of you so much. What would life have without you in it? The sun would drop from my heavens. I see only by you! you have kissed me on the eyes. You are more to me than my own poor brain could ever have devised: had I started to invent Paradise, I could not have invented *you*. But perhaps you have invented me: I am something new to myself since I saw you first. God bless you for it!

Even if you were to shut your eyes at me now —though I might go blind, you could not unmake me:—" The gods themselves cannot recall their gifts." Also that I am yours is a gift of the gods, I will trust: and so, not to be recalled!

Kiss me, dearest; here where I have written this! I am yours, Beloved. I kiss you again and again.—Ever your own making.

## LETTER XIX.

DEAREST, DEAREST: How long has this happened? You don't tell me the day or the
hour. Is it ever since you last wrote? Then
you have been in pain and grief for four days:
and I not knowing anything about it! And you
have no hand in the house kind enough to let
you dictate by it one small word to poor me?
What heartless merrymakings may I not have
sent you to worry you, when soothing was the
one thing wanted? Well, I will not worry now,
then; neither at not being told, nor at not being
allowed to come: but I will come thus and thus,
O my dear heart, and take you in my arms. And
you will be comforted, will you not be? when I
tell you that even if you had no legs at all, I
would love you just the same. Indeed, dearest,
so much of you is a superfluity: just your heart
against mine, and the sound of your voice, would
carry me up to more heavens than I could otherwise have dreamed of. I may say now, now
that I know it was not your choice, what a void
these last few days the lack of letters has been

to me.  I wondered, truly, if you had found it
well to put off such visible signs for a while in
order to appease one who, in other things more
essential, sees you rebellious.   But the wonder is
over now; and I don't want you to write—not
till a consultation of doctors orders it for the good
of your health.   I will be so happy talking to you:
also I am sending you books:—those I wish you
to read; and which now you *must,* since you have
the leisure!   And I for my part will make time
and read yours.   Whose do you most want me
to read, that my education in your likings may
become complete?   What I send you will not de-
prive me of anything: for I have the beautiful
complete set—your gift—and shall read side by
side with you to realize in imagination what the
happiness of reading them for the first time
ought to be.

Yesterday, by a most unsympathetic instinct,
I went out for a long tramp on my two feet; and
no ache in them came and told me of you!   Over
Sillingford I sat on a bank and looked downhill
where went a carter.   And I looked uphill
where lay something which might be nothing—
or not his.   Now, shall I make a fool of myself
by pursuing to tell him he may have dropped
something, or shall I go on and see?   So I went
on and saw a coat with a fat pocket: and by then
he was out of sight, and perhaps it wasn't his;

and it was very hot and the hill steep. So I minded my own business, making Cain's motto mine; and now feel so bad, being quite sure that it was his. And I wonder how many miles he will have tramped back looking for it, and whether his dinner was in the pocket.

These unintentional misdoings are the " sins " one repents of all one's life long: I have others stored away, the bitterest of small things done or undone in haste and repented of at so much leisure afterwards. And always done to people or things I had no grudge against, sometimes even a love for. They are my skeletons: I will tell you of them some day.

This, dearest, is our first enforced absence from each other; and I feel it almost more hard on me than on you. Beloved, let us lay our hearts together and get comforted. It is not real separation to know that another part of the world contains the rest of me. Oh, the rest of me, the rest of me that you are! So, thinking of you, I can never be tired. I rest yours.

## LETTER XX.

Yes, Dearest, " Patience!" but it is a virtue
I have little enough of naturally, and used to be
taught to pray for as a child. And I remember
once really hurting dear Mother-Aunt's feelings
by trying to repay her for that teaching by a little
iniquitous laughter at her expense. It was too
funny for me to feel very contrite about, as I do
sometimes over quite small things, or I would not
be telling it you now (for there are things in me
I would conceal even from you). I dare say you
wouldn't guess it, but the M.-A. is a most long
person over her private devotions. Perhaps it
was her own habit, with the cares of a household
sometimes conflicting, which made her recite to
me so often her pet legend of a saintly person who,
constantly interrupted over her prayers by mun-
dane matters, became a pattern in patience out of
these snippings of her godly desires. So, one
day, angels in the disguise of cross people with
selfish demands on her time came seeking to
know where in her composition or composure
exasperation began: and finding none, they let

her return in peace to her missal, where for a reward all the letters had been turned into gold. " And that, my dear, comes of patience," my aunt would say, till I grew a little tired of the saying. I don't know what experience my uncle had gathered of her patience under like circumstances: but I notice that to this day he treads delicately, like Agag, when he knows her to be on her knees; and prefers then to send me on his errands instead of doing them himself.

So it happened one day that he wanted a particular coat which had been put away in her clothes-closet—and she was on her knees between him and it, with the time of her Amen quite indefinite. I was sent, said my errand briefly, and was permitted to fumble out her keys from her pocket while she continued to kneel over her morning psalms.

What I brought to him turned out to be the wrong coat: I went back and knocked for readmittance. Long-suffering she bade me to come in. I explained, and still she repressed herself, only saying in a tone of affliction, " Do see this time that you take the right one ! "

After I had made my second selection, and proved it right on my uncle's person, the parallelism of things struck me, and I skipped back to my aunt's door and tapped. I got a low wailing "Yes?" for answer—a monosyllabic substitute for the " How long, O Lord? " of a saint in difficulties. When I called through the keyhole, " Are your psalms written in gold? " she became really angry:—I suppose because the miracle so well earned had not come to pass.

Well, dearest, if you have been patient with me over so much about nothing, I pray this letter may appear to you written in gold. Why I write so is, partly, that it is bad for us both to be down in the mouth, or with hearts down at heel: and so, since you cannot, I have to do the dancing:—and, partly, because I found I had a bad temper on me which needed curing, and being brought to the sun-go-down point of owing no man anything. Which, sooner said, has finally been done; and I am very meek now and loving to you, and everything belonging to you—not to come nearer the sore point.

And I hope some day, some day, as a reward to my present submission, that you will sprain your ankle in my company (just a very little bit for an excuse) and let me have the nursing of it! It hurts my heart to have your poor bones crying out for comfort that I am not to bring to them. I feel robbed of a part of my domestic training, and may never pick up what I have just lost. And I fear greatly you must have been truly in pain to have put off Meredith for a day. If I had been at hand to read to you, I flatter myself you would have liked him well, and been soothed. You must take the will, Beloved, for the deed. I kiss you now, as much as even you can demand; and when you get this I will be thinking of you all over again.—When do I ever leave off? Love, love, love till our next meeting, and then more love still, and more!—Ever your own.

## LETTER XXI.

DEAREST: I am in a simple mood to-day, and give you the benefit of it: I shall become complicated again presently, and you will hear from me directly that happens.

The house only emptied itself this morning; I may say emptied, for the remainder fits like a saint into her niche, and is far too comfortable to count. This is C——, whom you only once met, when she sat so much in the background that you will not remember her. She has one weakness, a thirst between meals—the blameless thirst of a rabid teetotaler. She hides cups of cold tea about the place, as a dog its bones: now and then one gets spilled or sat on, and when she hears of the accident, she looks thirsty, with a thirst which only *that* particular cup of tea could have quenched. In no other way is she any trouble: indeed, she is a great dear, and has the face of a Madonna, as beautiful as an apocryphal gospel to look at and " make believe " in.

Arthur, too, like the rest of them, when he came

over to give me his brotherly blessing, wished to know what you were like. I didn't pretend to remember your outward appearance too well,— told him you looked like a common or garden Englishman, and roused his suspicions by so careless a championship of my choice. He accused me of being in reality highly sentimental about you, and with having at that moment your portrait concealed and strung around my neck in a locket. Mother-Aunt stood up for me against him, declaring I was " too sensible a girl for nonsense of that sort." (It is a little weakness of hers, you know, to resent extremes of endearment towards anyone but herself in those she has " brooded," and she has thought us hitherto most restrained and proper—as, indeed, have we not been?) Arthur and I exchanged tokens of truce: in a little while off went my aunt to bed, leaving us alone. Then, for he is the one of us that I am most frank with: " Arthur," cried I, and up came your little locket like a bucket from a well, for him to have his first sight of you, my Beloved. He objected that he could not see faces in a nutshell; and I suppose others cannot: only I.

He, too, is gone. If you had been coming he would have spared another day—for to-day *was* planned and dated, you will remember—and we would have ridden halfway to meet you. But, as fate has tripped you, and made all comings on your part indefinite, he sends you his hopes for a later meeting.

How is your poor foot? I suppose, as it is ill, I may send it a kiss by post and wish it well? I do. Truly, you are to let me know if it gives you much pain, and I will lie awake thinking of you. This is not sentimental, for if one knows that a friend is occupied over one's sleeplessness one feels the comfort.

I am perplexed how else to give you my company: your mother, I know, could not yet truly welcome me; and I wish to be as patient as possible, and not push for favors that are not offered. So I cannot come and ask to take you out in *her* carriage, nor come and carry you away in mine. We must try how fast we can hold hands at a distance.

I have kept up to where you have been reading in " Richard Feverel," though it has been a scramble: for I have less opportunity of reading, I with my feet, than you without yours. In *your* book I have just got to the smuggling away of General Monk in the perforated coffin, and my sense of history capitulates in an abandonment of laughter. I yield! The Gaul's invasion of Britain always becomes broad farce when he attempts it. This in clever ludicrousness beats the unintentional comedy of Victor Hugo's " John-Jim-

Jack " as a name typical of Anglo-Saxon chris-
tenings. But Dumas, through a dozen absurdi-
ties, knows apparently how to stalk his quarry:
so large a genius may play the fool and remain
wise.

You see I have given your author a warm welcome at last: and what about you and mine?
Tell me you love his women and I will not be
jealous. Indeed, outside him I don't know where
to find a written English woman of modern times
whom I would care to meet, or could feel honestly bound to look up to:—nowhere will I have
her shaking her ringlets at me in Dickens or
Thackeray. Scott is simply not modern; and
Hardy's women, if they have nobility in them,
get so cruelly broken on the wheel that you get
but the wrecks of them at last. It is only his
charming baggages who come to a good ending.

I like an author who has the courage and self-
restraint to leave his noble creations alive: too
many try to ennoble them by death. For my
part, if I have to go out of life before you, I
would gladly trust you to the hands of Clara, or
Rose, or Janet, or most of all Vittoria; though,
to be accurate, I fear they have all grown too old
for you by now.

And you? have you any men to offer me in turn
out of your literary admirations, supposing you
should die of a snapped ankle? Would you give

me to d'Artagnan for instance? Hardly, I sus-
pect! But either choose me some proxy hero, or
get well and come to me! You will be very welcome when you do. Sleep is making sandy eyes
at me: good-night, dearest.

## LETTER XXII.

WHY, MY BELOVED: Since you put it to me as
a point of conscience (it is only lying on your back
with one active leg doing nothing, and the other
dying to have done aching, which has made you
take this new start of inquiring within upon
everything), since you call on me for a con-
scientious answer, I say that it stands to reason
that I love you more than you love me, because
there is so much more of you to love, let alone
fit for loving.

Do you imagine that you are going to be a crip-
ple for life, and therefore an indifferent dancer
in the dances I shall always be leading you,
that you have started this fit of self-depreciation?
Or is it because I have thrown Meredith at your
sick head that you doubt my tact and my affection, and my power patiently to bear for your
sake a good deal of cold shoulder? Dearest, remember I am doctoring you from a distance: and
am not yet allowed to come and see my patient,
so can only judge from your letters how ill you

are. That you have been concealing from me almost treacherously: and only by a piece of abject waylaying did I receive word to-day of your sleepless nights, and so get the key to your symptoms. Lay by Meredith, then, for a while: I am sending you a cargo of Stevenson instead. You have been truly unkind, trying to read what required effort, when you were fit for nothing of the sort.

And lest even Stevenson should be too much for you, and wanting very much, and perhaps a little bit jealously, to be your most successful nurse, I am letting my last large bit of shyness of you go; and with a pleasant sort of pain, because I know I have hit on a thing that will please you, I open my hands and let you have these, and with them goes my last blush: henceforth I am a woman without a secret, and all your interest in me may evaporate. Yet I know well it will not.

As for this resurrection pie from love's dead-letter office, you will find from it at least one thing—how much I depended upon response from you before I could become at all articulate. It is you, dearest, from the beginning who have set my head and heart free and made me a woman. I am something quite different from the sort of child I was less than a year ago when I wrote that small prayer which stands sponsor for all that follows. How abundantly it has been answered, dearest Beloved, only I know: you do not!

Now my prayer is not that you should " come true," but that you should get well. Do this one little thing for me, dearest! For you I will do anything: my happiness waits for that. As yet I seem to have done nothing. Oh, but, Beloved, I will! From a reading of the Fioretti, I sign myself as I feel.—Your glorious poor little one.

## THE CASKET LETTERS.

### A.

my dear Prince Wonderful,[1]

PRAY God bless —— —— and make him come true for my sake.   Amen.

R. S. V. P.

### B.

DEAR PRINCE WONDERFUL: Now that I have met you I pray that you will be my friend.   I want just a little of your friendship, but that, so much, so much!   And even for that little I do not know how to ask.

Always to be *your* friend: of that you shall be quite sure.

### C.

DEAR PRINCE WONDERFUL: Long ago when I was still a child I told myself of you: but thought of you only as in a fairy tale.   Now I am afraid of trusting my eyes or ears, for fear I should

---

[1] The MS. contained at first no name, but a blank ; over it this has been written afterwards in a small hand.

think too much of you before I know you really
to be true.   Do not make me wish so much to be
your friend, unless you are also going to be true!

Please come true now, for mine and for all the
world's sake:—but for mine especially, because I
thought of you first!   And if you are not able to
come true, don't make me see you any more.   I
shall always remember you, and be glad that I
have seen you just once.

### D.

DEAR PRINCE WONDERFUL: *Has* God blessed
you yet and made you come true?   I have not
seen you again, so how am I to know?   Not that
it is necessary for me to know even if you do come
true.   I believe already that you are true.

If I were never to see you again I should be
glad to think of you as living, and shall always
be your friend.   I pray that you may come to
know that.

### E.

DEAR HIGHNESS: I do not know what to write
to you: I only know how much I wish to write.
I have always written the things I thought about:
it has been easy to find words for them.   Now I
think about you, but have no words:—no words,

dear Highness, for you! I could write at once if I knew you were my friend. Come true for me: I will have so much to tell you then!

## F.

Dear Highness: If I believe in fairy tales coming true, it is because I am superstitious. This is what I did to-day. I shut my eyes and took a book from the shelf, opened it, and put my fingers down on a page. This is what I came to:

> " All I believed is true !
>   I am able yet
>   All I want to get
>  By a method as strange as new:
>  Dare I trust the same to you ?"

Fate says, then, you are to be my friend. Fate has said I am yours already. That is very certain. Only in real life where things come true would a book have opened as this has done.

## G.

Dear Highness: I am sure now, then, that I please you, and that you like me, perhaps only a little: for you turned out of your way to ride with me though you were going somewhere so fast. How much I wished it when I saw you coming, but dared not believe it would come true!

"Come true": it is the word I have always been writing, and everything *has*:—you most of all! You are more true each time I see you. So true that now I will write it down at last,—the truth for you who have come so true.

Dear Highness and Great Heart, I love you dearly, though you don't know it,—quite ever so much; and am going to love you ever so much more, only—please like *me* a little better first! You on your dear side must do something: or, before I know, I may be wringing my hands all alone on a desert island to a bare blue horizon, with nothing in it real or fabulous.

If I am to love you, nothing but happiness is to be allowed to come of it. So don't come true too fast without one little wee corresponding wish for me to find that you are! I am quite happy thinking you out slowly: it takes me all day long; the longer the better!

I wonder how often in my life I shall write down that I love you, having once written it (I do:—I love you! there [it] is for you, with more to follow after!); and send you my love as I do now into the great emptiness of chance, hoping somehow, known or unknown, it may bless you and bring good to you.

Oh, but 'tis a windy world, and I a mere

feather in it: how can I get blown the way I would?

Still I have a superstition that some star is over me which I have not seen yet, but shall,—Heaven helping me.

And now good-night, and no more, no more at all! I send out an " I love you " to be my celestial commercial traveler for me while I fold myself up and become its sleeping partner.

Good-night: you are the best and truest that I ever dreamed yet.

### H.

DEAR HIGHNESS: I begin not to be able to name you anything, for there is not a word for you that will do! " Highness " you are: but that leaves gaps and coldnesses without end. " Royal," yet much more serene than royal: though by that I don't mean any detraction from your royalty, for I never saw a man carry his invisible crown with so level a head and no haughtiness at all: and that is the finest royalty of look possible.

I look at you and wonder so how you have grown to this—to have become king so quietly without any coronation ceremony. You have thought more than you should for happiness at your age; making me, by that one line in your forehead, think you were three years older than

you really are. I wish—if I dare wish you anything different—that you were! It makes me
uncomfortable to remember that I am—what?
Almost half a year your elder as time flies:—
not really, for your brain was born long before
mine began to rattle in its shell. You say quite
*old* things, and quietly, as if you had had them in
your mind ten years already. When you told me
about your two old pensioners, the blind man and
his wife, whom you brought to so funny a reconciliation, I felt ("mir war, ich wuszte nicht
wie") that I would like very much to go blind-
fold led by you: it struck me suddenly how
happy would be a blindfoldness of perfect trust
such as one might have with your hands on one.
I suppose that is what in religion is called faith:
I haven't it there, my dear; but I have it in you
now. I love you, beginning to understand why:
at first I did not. I am ashamed not to have
discovered it earlier. The matter with you is that
you have goodness prevailing in you, an integrity
of goodness, I mean:—a different thing from
there being a whereabouts for goodness in you;
*that* we all have in some proportion or another.
I was quite right to love you: I know it now,—I
did not when I first did.

Yesterday I was turning over a silly "confession book" in which a rose was everybody's favorite flower, manliness the finest quality for a

man, and womanliness for a woman (which is as
much as to say that pig is the best quality for
pork, and pork for pig) : till I came upon one
different from the others, and found myself saying " Yes " all down the page.

I turned over for the signature, and found my
own mother's.   Was it not a strange sweet meeting?   And only then did the memory of her
handwriting from far back come to me.   She
died, dear Highness, before I was seven years
old.   I love her as I do my early memory of
flowers, as something very sweet, hardly as a
real person.

I noticed she loved best in men and women
what they lack most often : in a man, a fair mind ;
in a woman, courage.   " Brave women and fair
men," she wrote.   Byron might have turned in
his grave at having his dissolute stiff-neck so
wrung for him by misquotation.   And she—it
must have been before the eighties had started the
popular craze for him—chose Meredith, my own
dear Meredith, for her favorite author.   How
our tastes would have run together had she lived !

Well, I know you fair, and believe myself brave
—constitutionally, so that I can't help it : and this,
therefore, is not self-praise.   But fairness in a
man is a deadly hard acquirement, I begin now
to discover.   You have it fixed fast in you.

You, I think, began to do just things con-

sciously, as the burden of manhood began in you.
I love to think of you growing by degrees till you
could carry your head *so*—and no other way;
so that, looking at you, I can promise myself you
never did a mean thing, and never consciously an
unjust thing except to yourself. I can just fancy
that fault in you. But, whatever—I love you
for it more and more, and am proud knowing you
and finding that we are to become friends. For
it is that, and no less than that, now.

I love you; and me you like cordially: and that
is enough. I need not look behind it, for already
I have no way to repay you for the happiness this
brings me.

## I.

OH, I think greatly of you, my dear; and it
takes long thinking. Not merely such a quantity
of thought, but such a quality, makes so hard a
day's work that by the end of it I am quite
drowsy. Bless me, dearest; all to-day has be-
longed to you; and to-morrow, I know, waits to
become yours without the asking: just as without the asking I too am yours. I wish it were
more possible for us to give service to those we
love. I am most glad because I see you so
often: but I come and go in your life empty-
handed, though I have so much to give away.
Thoughts, the best I have, I give you: I cannot

empty my brain of them. Some day you shall think well of me.—That is a vow, dear friend,— you whom I love so much!

## J.

I HAVE not had to alter any thought ever formed about you, Beloved; I have only had to deepen it—that is all. You grow, but you remain. I have heard people talk about you, generally kindly; but what they think of you is often wrong. I do not say anything, but I am glad, and so sure that I know you better. If my mind is so clear about you, it shows that you are good for me. Now for nearly three months I may not see you again; but all that time you will be growing in my heart; and at the end without another word from you I shall find that I know you better than before. Is that strange? It is because I love you: love is knowledge—blind knowledge, not wanting eyes. I only hope that I shall keep in your memory the kind place you have given me. You are almost my friend now, and I know it. You do not know that I love you.

## K.

BELOVED: You love me! I know it now, and bless the sun and the moon and the stars for the dear certainty of it. And I ask you now,

O heart that has opened to me, have I once been
unhappy or impatient while this good thing has
been withheld from me? Indeed my love for
you has occupied me too completely: I have
been so glad to find how much there is to learn
in a good heart deeply unconscious of its own
goodness. You have employed me as I wish I
may be employed all the days of my life: and
now my beloved employer has given me the
wages I did not ask.

You love me! Is it a question of little or
much? Is it not rather an entire new thought
of me that has entered your life, as the thought
of you entered mine months that seem years ago?
It was the seed then, and seemed small; but the
whole life was there; and it has grown and
grown till now it is I who have become small,
and have hardly room in me for the roots: and
it seems to have gone so far up over my head
that I wonder if the stars know of my happiness.

They must know of yours too, then, my Beloved: they are no company for me without you.
Oh, to-day, to-day of all days! how in my heart
I shall go on kissing it till I die! You love me:
that is wonderful! You love me: and already it
is not wonderful in the least! but belongs to
Noah and the ark and all the animals saved up
for an earth washed clean and dried, and the new
beginnings of time which have ever since been

twisting and turning with us in safe keeping through all the history of the world.

" We came over at the Norman conquest," my dear, as people say trailing their pedigree: but there was no ancestral pride about us—it was all for the love of the thing we did it: how clear it seems now! In the hall hangs a portrait in a big wig, but otherwise the image of my father, of a man who flouted the authority of James II. merely because he was so like my father in character that he could do nothing else. I shall look for you now in the Bayeux tapestries with a prong from your helmet down the middle of your face—of which that line on your forehead is the remainder. And you love me! I wonder what the line has to do with that?

By such little things do great things seem to come about: not really. I know it was not because I said just what I did say, and did what I did yesterday, that your heart was bound to come for mine. But it was those small things that brought you consciousness: and when we parted I knew that I had all the world at my feet—or all heaven over my head!

Ah, at last I may let the spirit of a kiss go to you from me, and not be ashamed or think myself forward since I have your love. All this time you are thinking of me: a certainty lying far outside what I can see.

Beloved, if great happiness may be set to any words, it is here! If silence goes better with it, —speak, silence, for me when I end now!

Good-night, and think greatly of me! I shall wake early.

## L.

Dearest: Was my heart at all my own,—was it my own to give, till you came and made me aware of how much it contains? Truly, dear, it contained nothing before, since now it contains you and nothing else. So I have a brand-new heart to give away: and you, you want it and can't see that there it is staring you in the face like a rose with all its petals ready to drop.

I am quite sure that if I had not met you, I could have loved nobody as I love you. Yet it is very likely that I should have loved—sufficiently, as the way of the world goes. It is not a romantic confession, but it is true to life: I do so genuinely like most of my fellow-creatures, and am not happy except where shoulders rub socially:—that is to say, have not until now been happy, except dependently on the company and smiles of others. Now, Beloved, I have none of your company, and have had but few of your smiles (I could count them all); yet I have become more happy filling up my solitude with the understanding of you which has made me wise, than all the rest of fate or fortune could make me.   Down comes autumn's sad heart and finds me gay; and the asters, which used to chill me at their appearing, have come out like crocuses this year because it is the beginning of a new world.

And all the winter will carry more than a suspicion of summer with it, just as the longest days carry round light from northwest to northeast, because so near the horizon, but out of sight, lies their sun.   So you, Beloved, so near to me now at last, though out of sight.

M.

Beloved: Whether I have sorry or glad things to think about, they are accompanied and changed by thoughts of you.   You are my diary: —all goes to you now.   That you love me is the very light by which I see everything.   Also I learn so much through having you in my thoughts: I cannot say how it is, for I have no more knowledge of life than I had before:—yet I am wiser, I believe, knowing much more what lives at the root of things and what men have meant and felt in all they have done:—because I love you, dearest.   Also I am quicker in my apprehensions, and have more joy and more fear in me than I had before. And if this seems to be all about myself, it is all about you really, Beloved!

Last week one of my dearest old friends, our Rector, died: a character you too would have loved. He was a father to the whole village, rather stern of speech, and no respecter of persons. Yet he made a very generous allowance for those who did not go through the church door to find their salvation. I often went only because I loved him: and he knew it.

I went for that reason alone last Sunday. The whole village was full of closed blinds: and of all things over him Chopin's Funeral March was played!—a thing utterly unchristian in its meaning: wild pagan grief, desolate over lost beauty. "Balder the beautiful is dead, is dead!" it cried: and I thought of you suddenly; you, who are not Balder at all. Too many thorns have been in your life, but not the mistletoe stroke dealt by a blind god ignorantly. Yet in all great joy there is the Balder element: and I feared lest something might slay it for me, and my life become a cry like Chopin's march over mown-down unripened grass, and youth slain in its high places.

After service a sort of processional instinct drew people up to the house: they waited about till permission was given, and went in to look at their

old man, lying in high state among his books.    I
did not go.  Beloved, I have never yet seen
death: you have, I know.  Do you, I wonder,
remember your father better than I mine:—or
your brother?  Are they more living because
you saw them once not living?  I think death
might open our eyes to those we lived on ill
terms with, but not to the familiar and dear.  I
do not need you dead, to be certain that your
heart has mine for its true inmate and mine
yours.

I love you, I love you: so let good-night bring
you good-morning!

### N.

At long intervals, dearest, I write to you a
secret all about yourself for my eyes to see: because, chiefly because, I have not you to look
at.  Thus I bless myself with you.

Away over the world west of this and a little
bit north is the city of spires where you are now.
Never having seen it I am the more free to picture it as I like: and to me it is quite full of
you:—quite greedily full, Beloved, when elsewhere you are so much wanted!  I send my
thoughts there to pick up crumbs for me.

It is a strange blend of notions—wisdom and
ignorance combined: for *you* I seem to know

perfectly; but of your life nothing at all. And yet nobody there knows so much about you as I. What you *do* matters so much less than what you are. You, who are the dearest heart in all the world, do what you will, you are so still to me, Beloved.

I take a happy armful of thoughts about you into all my dreams: and when I wake they are there still, and have done nothing but remain true. What better can I ask of them?

You do love me: you have not changed? Without change I remain yours so long as I live.

### O.

AND you, Beloved, what are you thinking of me all this while? Think well of me, I beg you: I deserve so much, loving you as truly as I do!

So often, dearest, I sit thinking my hands into yours again as when we were saying good-by the last time. Then it was, under our laughter and light words, that I saw suddenly how the thing too great to name had become true, that from friends we were changed into lovers. It seemed the most natural thing to be, and yet was wonderful—for it was I who loved you first: a thing I could never be ashamed of, and am now proud to own—for has it not proved me wise? My love for you is the best wisdom that I have.

Good-night, dearest! Sleep as well as I love you, and nobody in the world will sleep so soundly.

### P.

A FEW times in my life, Beloved, I have had the Blue-moon-hunger for something which seemed too impossible and good ever to come true: prosaic people call it being " in the blues "; I comfort myself with a prettier word for it. To-day, not the Blue-moon itself, but the Man of it came down and ate plum-porridge with me! Also, I do believe that it burnt his mouth, and am quite reasonably happy thinking so, since it makes me know that you love me as much as ever.

If I have had doubts, dearest, they have been of myself, lest I might be unworthy of your friendship or love. Suspicions of you I never had.

Who wrote that suspicions among thoughts are like bats among birds, flying only by twilight?

But even my doubts have been thoughts, Beloved,—sure of you if not always of myself. And if I have looked for you only with doubtful vision, yet I have always seen you in as strong a light as my eyes could bear:—blue-moonlight,

Beloved, is not twilight: and blue-moonlight has been the light I saw you by: it is you alone who can make sunlight of it.

This I read yesterday has lain on my mind since as true and altogether beautiful, with the beauty of major, not of minor poetry, though it was a minor poet who wrote it. It is of a wood where Apollo has gone in quest of his Beloved, and she is not yet to be found:

> " Here each branch
> Swayed with a glitter all its crowded leaves,
> And brushed the soft divine hair touching them
> In ruffled clusters. . . .
> Suddenly the moon
> Smoothed herself out of vapor-drift and made
> The deep night full of pleasure in the eye
> Of her sweet motion. Not alone she came
> Leading the starlight with her like a song:
> And not a bud of all that undergrowth
> But crisped and tingled out an ardent edge
> As the light steeped it : over whose massed leaves
> The portals of illimitable sleep
> Faded in heaven."

That is love in its moonrise, not its sunrise stage: yet you see, Beloved, how it takes possession of its dark world, quite as fully as the brighter sunlight could do. And if I speak of doubts, I mean no twilight and no suspicions: nor by darkness do I mean any unhappiness.

My blue-moon has come, leading the starlight

with her like a song.   Am I not happy enough
to be patiently yours before you know it?   Good
things which are to be, before they happen are
already true.   Nothing is so true as you are, except my love for you and yours for me.   Good-
night, good-night.

Sleep well, Beloved, and wake.


## Q.

BELOVED: I heard somebody yesterday speak
of you as " charming "; and I began wondering
to myself was that the word which could ever
have covered my thoughts of you?   I do not
know whether you ever charmed me, except in
the sense of charming which means magic and
spell-binding.   *That* you did from the beginning,
dearest.   But I think I held you at first in too
much awe to discover charm in you: and at last
knew you too much to the depths to name you
by a word so lightly used for the surface of
things.   Yet now a charm in you, which is not
*all* you, but just a part of you, comes to light,
when I see you wondering whether you are really
loved, or whether, Beloved, I only *like* you rather
well!

Well, if you will be so " charming," I am helpless: and can do nothing, nothing, but pray for
the blue-moon to rise, and love you a little better

because you have some of that divine foolishness which strikes the very wise ones of earth, and makes them kin to weaker mortals who otherwise might miss their " charm " altogether.

Truly, Beloved, if I am happy, it is because I am also your most patiently loving.

R.

BELOVED: The certainty which I have now that you love me so fills all my thoughts, I cannot understand you being in any doubt on your side. What must I do that I do not do, to show gladness when we meet and sorrow when we have to part? I am sure that I make no pretense or disguise, except that I do not stand and wring my hands before all the world, and cry " Don't go! "—which has sometimes been in my mind, to be kept *not* said!

Indeed, I think so much of you, my dear, that I believe some day, if you do your part, you will only have to look up from your books to find me standing. If you did, would you still be in doubt whether I loved you?

Oh, if any apparition of me ever goes to you, all my thoughts will surely look truthfully out of its eyes; and even you will read what is there at last!

Beloved, I kiss your blind eyes, and love them

the better for all their unreadiness to see that I am already their slave. Not a day now but I think I may see you again: I am in a golden uncertainty from hour to hour.

I love you: you love me: a mist of blessing swims over my eyes as I write the words, till they become one and the same thing: I can no longer divide their meaning in my mind. Amen: there is no need that I should.

## S.

Beloved: I have not written to you for quite a long time: ah, I could not. I have nothing now to say! I think I could very easily die of this great happiness, so certainly do you love me! Just a breath more of it and I should be gone.

Good-by, dearest, and good-by, and good-by! If you want letters from me now, you must ask for them! That the earth contains us both, and that we love each other, is about all that I have mind enough to take in. I do not think I can love you more than I do: you are no longer my dream but my great waking thought. I am waiting for no blue-moonrise now: my heart has not a wish which you do not fulfill. I owe you my whole life, and for any good to you must pay it out to the last farthing, and still feel myself your debtor.

Oh, Beloved, I am most poor and most rich when I think of your love. Good-night; I can never let thought of you go!

―――――

BELOVED: These are almost all of them, but not quite; a few here and there have cried to be taken out, saying they were still too shy to be looked at. I can't argue with them: they know their own minds best; and you know mine.

See what a dignified historic name I have given this letter-box, or chatterbox, or whatever you like to call it. But " Resurrection Pie " is *my* name for it. Don't eat too much of it, prays your loving.

## LETTER XXIII.

Saving your presence, dearest, I would rather have Prince Otto, a very lovable character for second affections to cling to. Richard Feverel would never marry again, so I don't ask for him: as for the rest, they are all too excellent for me. They give me the impression ·of having worn copy-books under their coats, when they were boys, to cheat punishment: and the copy-books got beaten into their systems.

You must find me somebody who was a " gallous young hound " in the days of his youth —Crossjay, for instance:—there! I have found the very man for me!

But really and truly, are you better? It will not hurt your foot to come to me, since I am not to come to you? How I long to see you again, dearest! it is an age! As a matter of fact, it is a fortnight: but I dread lest you will find some change in me. I have kept a real white hair to show you, I drew it out of my comb the other morning: wound up into a curl it becomes quite visible, and it is ivory-white:

you are not to think it flaxen, and take away its one wee sentiment! And I make you an offer: —you shall have it if, honestly, you can find in your own head a white one to exchange.

Dearest, I am not *hurt,* nor do I take seriously to heart your mother's present coldness. How much more I could forgive her when I put myself in her place! She may well feel a struggle and some resentment at having to give up in any degree her place with you. All my selfishness would come to the front if that were demanded of me.

Do not think, because I leave her alone, that I am repaying her coldness in the same coin. I know that for the present anything I do must offend. Have I demanded your coming too soon? Then stay away another day—or two: every day only piles up the joy it will be to have your arms round me once more. I can keep for a little longer: and the gray hair will keep, and many to-morrows will come bringing good things for us, when perhaps your mother's "share of the world" will be over.

Don't say it, but when you next kiss her, kiss her for me also: I am sorry for all old people: their love of things they are losing is so far more to be reverenced and made room for than ours of the things which will come to us in good time abundantly.

To-night I feel selfish at having too much of your love: and not a bit of it can I let go! I hope, Beloved, we shall live to see each other's gray hairs in earnest: gray hairs that we shall not laugh at, as at this one I pulled. How dark your dear eyes will look with a white setting! My heart's heart, every day you grow larger round me, and I so much stronger depending upon you!

I won't say—come for certain, to-morrow: but come if, and as soon as, you can. I seem to see a mile further when I am on the lookout for you: and I shall be long-sighted every day until you come. It is only *doubtful* hope deferred which maketh the heart sick. I am as happy as the day is long waiting for you: but the day *is* long, dearest, none the less when I don't see you.

All this space on the page below is love. I have no time left to put it into words, or words into it. You bless my thoughts constantly.— Believe me, never your thoughtless.

## LETTER XXIV.

DEAREST: How, when, and where is there any use wrangling as to which of us loves the other the best (" the better," I believe, would be the more grammatical phrase in incompetent Queen's English), and why in that of all things should we pretend to be rivals?· For this at least seems certain to me, that, being created male and female, no two lovers since the world began ever loved each other quite in the *same* way: it is not in nature for it to be so. They cannot compare: only to the best that is in them they *do* love each after their kind,—as do we for certain!

Be sure, then, that I am utterly contented with what I get (and you, Beloved, and you?): nay, I wonder forever at the love you have given me: and if I will to lay mine at your feet, and feel yours crowning my life,—why, so it is, you know; you cannot alter it! And if you insist that your love is at *my* feet, I have only to turn Irish and reply that it is because I am heels over head in love with you:—and, mark you, that is no pretty attitude for a lady that you have driven me into in order that I may stick to my " crown "!

Go to, dearest! There is one thing in which I can beat you, and that is in the bandying of words and all verbal conjurings: take this as the last proof of it and rest quiet. I know you love me a great great deal more than I have wit or power to love you: and that is just the little reason why your love mounts till, as I tell you, it crowns me (head or heels): while mine, insufficient and groveling, lies at your feet, and will till they become amputated. And I can give you, but won't, sixty other reasons why things are as I say, and are to be left as I say. And oh, my world, my world, it is with you I go round sunwards, and you make my evenings and mornings, and will, till Time shuts his wings over us! And now it is doleful business I have to write to you. . .

I have dropped to sleep over all this writing of things, and my cheek down on the page has made the paper unwilling to take the ink again: —what a pretty compliment to me: and, if you prefer it, what an easy way of writing to you! I can send you such any day and be as idle as I like. And you will decide about all the above exactly as you and I think best (or should it be " better " again, being only between us two?).

When you get this, blow your beloved self a kiss in the glass for me,—a great big shattering blow that shall astonish Mercury behind his window-pane. Good-night, my best—or "better," for that is what I most want you to be.

## LETTER XXV.

MY OWN BELOVED: And I never thanked you yesterday for your dear words about the resurrection pie; that comes of quarreling! Well, you must prove them and come quickly that I may see this restoration of health and spirits that you assure me of. You avoid saying that they sent you to sleep; but I suppose that is what you mean.

Fate meant me only to light upon gay things this morning: listen to this and guess where it comes from:

> "When March with variant winds was past,
> And April had with her silver showers
> Ta'en leif at life with an orient blast ;
> And lusty May, that mother of flowers,
> Had made the birds to begin their hours,
> Among the odours ruddy and white,
> Whose harmony was the ear's delight :

> "In bed at morrow I sleeping lay ;
> Methought Aurora, with crystal een,
> In at the window looked by day,
> And gave me her visage pale and green:
> And on her hand sang a lark from the splene,
> 'Awake ye lovers from slumbering !
> See how the lusty morrow doth spring !' "

Ah, but you are no scholar of the things in your own tongue! That is Dunbar, a Scots poet contemporary of Henry VII., just a little bit altered by me to make him soundable to your ears. If I had not had to leave an archaic word here and there, would you ever have guessed he lay outside this century? That shows the permanent element in all good poetry, and in all good joy in things also. In the four centuries since that was written we have only succeeded in worsening the meaning of certain words, as for instance "spleen," which now means irritation and vexation, but stood then for quite the opposite—what we should call, I suppose, "a full heart." It is what I am always saying—a good digestion is the root of nearly all the good living and high thinking we are capable of: and the spleen was then the root of the happy emotions as it is now of the miserable ones. Your pre-Reformation lark sang from "a full stomach," and thanked God it had a constitution to carry it off without affectation: and your nineteenth century lark applying the same code of life, his plain-song is mere happy everyday prose, and not poetry at all as we try to make it out to be.

I have no news for you at all of anyone: all inside the house is a simmer of peace and quiet, with blinds drawn down against the heat the whole day long. No callers; and as for me, I never call elsewhere. The gossips about here eke out a precarious existence by washing each other's dirty linen in public: and the process never seems to result in any satisfactory cleansing.

I avoid saying what news I trust to-morrow's post-bag may contain for me. Every wish I send you comes "from the spleen," which means I am very healthy, and, conditionally, as happy as is good for me. Pray God bless my dear Share of the world, and make him get well for his own and my sake! Amen.

This catches the noon post, an event which always shows I am jubilant, with a lot of the opposite to a "little death" feeling running over my nerves. I feel the grass growing *under* me: the reverse of poor Keats' complaint. Good-by, Beloved, till I find my way into the provender of to-morrow's post-bag.

## LETTER XXVI.

OH, wings of the morning, here you come! I have been looking out for you ever since post came. Roberts is carrying orders into town, and will bring you this with a touch of the hat and an amused grin under it. I saw you right on the top Sallis Hill: this is to wager that my eyes have told me correctly. Look out for me from far away, I am at my corner window: wave to me! Dearest, this is to kiss you before I can.

## LETTER XXVII.

DEAREST: I have made a bad beginning of the
week: I wonder how it will end? it all comes of
my not seeing enough of you. Time hangs
heavy on my hands, and the Devil finds me the
mischief!

I prevailed upon myself to go on Sunday and
listen to our new lately appointed vicar: for I
thought it not fair to condemn him on the
strength of Mrs. P——'s terrible reporting
powers and her sensuous worship of his full-
blown flowers of speech—" pulpit-pot-plants " is
what I call them.

It was not worse and not otherwise than I
had expected. I find there are only two kinds
of clerics as generally necessary to salvation in
a country parish—one leads his parishioners to
the altar and the other to the pulpit: and the
latter is vastly the more popular among the articulate and gad-about members of his flock.
This one sways himself over the edge of his
frame, making signals of distress in all directions,
and with that and his windy flights of oratory

suggests twenty minutes in a balloon-car, till he comes down to earth at the finish with the Doxology for a parachute. His shepherd's crook is one long note of interrogation, with which he tries to hook down the heavens to the understanding of his hearers, and his hearers up to an understanding of himself. All his arguments are put interrogatively, and few of them are worth answering. Well, well, I shall be all the freer for your visit when you come next Sunday, and any Sunday after that you will: and he shall come in to tea if you like and talk to you in quite a cultured and agreeable manner, as he can when his favorite beverage is before him.

I discover that I get "the snaps" on a Monday morning, if I get them at all. The M.-A. gets them on the Sunday itself, softly but regularly: they distress no one, and we all know the cause: her fingers are itching for the knitting which she mayn't do. Your Protestant ignores Lent as a Popish device, a fond thing vainly invented: but spreads it instead over fifty-two days in the year. Why, I want to know, cannot I change the subject?

Sunday we get no post (and no collection except in church) unless we send down to the town for it, so Monday is all the more welcome: but this I have been up and writing before it arrives —therefore the "snaps."

Our postman is a lovely sight. I watched him walking up the drive the other morning, and he seemed quite perfection, for I guessed he was bringing me the thing which would make me happy all day. I only hope the Government pays him properly.

I think this is the least pleasant letter I have ever sent you: shall I tell you why? It was not the sermon: he is quite a forgivable good man in his way. But in the afternoon that same Mrs. P—— came, got me in a corner, and wanted to unburden herself of invective against your mother, believing that I should be glad, because her coldness to me has become known! What mean things some people can think about one! I heard nothing: but I am ruffled in all my plumage and want stroking. And my love to your mother, please, if she will have it. It is only through her that I get you.—Ever your very own.

## LETTER XXVIII.

DEAREST: Here comes a letter to you from me flying in the opposite direction. I won't say I am not wishing to go; but oh, to be a bird in two places at once! Give this letter, then, a special nesting-place, because I am so much on the wing elsewhere.

I shut my eyes most of the time through France, and opened them on a soup-tureen full of coffee which presented itself at the frontier: and then realized that only a little way ahead lay Berne, with baths, buns, bears, breakfast, and other nice things beginning with B, waiting to make us clean, comfortable, contented, and other nice things beginning with C.

Through France I loved you sleepy fashion, with many dreams in between not all about you. But now I am breathing thoughts of you out of a new atmosphere—a great gulp of you, all clean-living and high-thinking between these Alpine royal highnesses with snow-white crowns to their heads: and no time for a word more about anything except you: you, and double-you,

—and treble-you if the alphabet only had grace to contain so beautiful a symbol!  Good-by: we meet next, perhaps, out of Lucerne: if not,— Italy.

What a lot I have to go through before we meet again visibly!  You will find me world-worn, my Beloved!  Write often.

## LETTER XXIX.

BELOVED: You know of the method for making a cat settle down in a strange place by buttering her all over: the theory being that by the time she has polished off the butter she feels herself at home? My morning's work has been the buttering of the Mother-Aunt with such things as will Lucerne her the most. When her instincts are appeased I am the more free to indulge my own.

So after breakfast we went round the cloisters, very thick set with tablets and family vaults, and crowded graves inclosed. It proved quite " the best butter." To me the penance turned out interesting after a period of natural repulsion. A most unpleasant addition to sepulchral sentiment is here the fashion: photographs of the departed set into the stone. You see an elegant and genteel marble cross: there on the pedestal above the name is the photo:—a smug man with bourgeois whiskers,—a militiaman with waxed mustaches well turned up,—a woman well attired and conscious of it: you cannot think how indecent looked the pretension of such types to the dignity of death and immortality.

But just one or two faces stood the test, and were justified: a young man oppressed with the burden of youth; a sweet, toothless grandmother in a bonnet, wearing old age like a flower; a woman not beautiful but for her neck which carried indignation; her face had a thwarted look. " Dead and rotten " one did not say of these in disgust and involuntarily as one did of the others. And yet I don't suppose the eye picks out the faces that kindled most kindness round them when living, or that one can see well at all where one sees without sympathy.    I think the Mother-Aunt's face would not look dear to most people as it does to me,—yet my sight of her is the truer: only I would not put it up on a tombstone in order that it might look nothing to those that pass by.

I wrote this much, and then, leaving the M.-A. to glory in her innumerable correspondence, Arthur and I went off to the lake, where we have been for about seven hours.    On it, I found it become infinitely more beautiful, for everything was mystified by a lovely bloomy haze, out of which the white peaks floated like dreams: and the mountains change and change, and seem not all the same as going when returning.    Don't ask me to write landscape to you: one breathes it in, and it is there ever after, but remains unset to words.

The T——s whittle themselves out of our company just to the right amount: come back at the right time (which is more than Arthur and I are likely to do when our legs get on the spin), and are duly welcome with a diversity of doings to talk about. Their tastes are more the M.-A.'s, and their activities about halfway between hers and ours, so we make rather a fortunate quintette. The M—— trio join us the day after to-morrow, when the majority of us will head away at once to Florence. Arthur growls and threatens he means to be left behind for a week: and it suits the funny little jealousy of the M.-A. well enough to see us parted for a time, quite apart from the fact that I shall then be more dependent on her company. She will then glory in overworking herself,—say it is me; and I shall feel a fiend. No letter at all, dearest, this; merely talky-talky.—Yours without words.

## LETTER XXX.

DEAREST: I cannot say I have seen Pisa, for the majority had their way, and we simply skipped into it, got ourselves bumped down at the Duomo and Campo Santo for two hours, fell exhausted to bed, and skipped out again by the first train next morning. Over the walls of the Campo Santo are some divine crumbs of Benozzo Gozzoli (don't expect me ever to spell the names of dead painters correctly: it is a politeness one owes to the living, but the famous dead are exalted by being spelt phonetically as the heart dictates, and become all the better company for that greatest of unspelled and spread-about names—Shakspere, Shakspeare, Shakespeare— his mark, not himself). Such a long parenthesis requires stepping-stones to carry you over it: " crumbs " was the last (wasn't a whole loaf of bread a stepping-stone in one of Andersen's fairy-tales?): but, indeed, I hadn't time to digest them properly. Let me come back to them before I die, and bury me in that inclosure if you love me as much then as I think you do now.

CAMPO SANTO, PISA.    P. 114.

The Baptistry has a roof of echoes that is wonderful,—a mirror of sound hung over the head of an official who opens his mouth for centimes to drop there. You sing notes up into it (or rather you don't, for that is his perquisite), and they fly circling, and flock, and become a single chord stretching two octaves: till you feel that you are living inside what in the days of our youth would have been called " the sound of a grand Amen."

The cathedral has fine points, or more than points—aspects: but the Italian version of Gothic, with its bands of flat marbles instead of moldings, was a shock to me at first. I only begin to understand it now that I have seen the outside of the Duomo at Florence. Curiously enough, it doesn't strike me as in the least Christian, only civic and splendid, reminding me of what Ruskin says about church architecture being really a dependant on the feudal or domestic. The Strozzi Palace is a beautiful piece of street-architecture; its effect is of an iron hand which gives you a buffet in the face when you look up and wonder—how shall I climb in? I will tell you more about insides when I write next.

I fear my last letter to you from Lucerne may either have strayed, or not even have begun straying: for in the hurry of coming away I left it, addressed, I *think*, but unstamped; and I am not sure that that particular hotel will be Christian enough to spare the postage out of the bill, which had a galaxy of small extras running into centimes, and suggesting a red-tape rectitude that would not show blind twenty-five-centime gratitude to the backs of departed guests.  So be patient and forgiving if I seem to have written little.  I found two of yours waiting for me, and cannot choose between them which I find most dear.  I will say, for a fancy, the shorter, that you may ever be encouraged to write your shortest rather than none at all.  One word from you gives me almost as much pleasure as twenty, for it contains all your sincerity and truth; and what more do I want?  You bless me quite.  How many perfectly happy days I owe to you, and seldom dare dream that I have made any beginning of a return!  If I could take one unhappy day out of your life, dearest, the secret would be mine, and no such thing should be left in it.  Be happy, beloved! oh, happy, happy,— with me for a partial reason—that is what I wish!

## LETTER XXXI.

DEAREST: The Italian paper-money paralyzes my brain: I cannot calculate in it; and were I left to myself an unscrupulous shopman could empty me of pounds without my becoming conscious of it till I beheld vacuum. But the T——s have been wonderful caretakers to me: and to-morrow Arthur rejoins us, so that I shall be able to resume my full activities under his safe-conduct.

The ways of the Italian cabbies and porters fill me with terror for the time when I may have to fall alive and unassisted into their hands: they have neither conscience nor gratitude, and regard thievish demands when satisfied merely as stepping-stones to higher things.

Many of the outsides of Florence I seemed to know by heart—the Palazzo Vecchio for instance. But close by it Cellini's two statues, the Judith and the Perseus, brought my heart up to my mouth unexpectedly. The Perseus is so out of proportion as to be ludicrous from one point of view: but another is magnificent enough to make me forgive the scamp his autobiography from now to the day of judgment (when we shall all begin forgiving each other in great haste, I suppose, for fear of the devil taking the hindmost!), and I registered a vow on the spot to that effect:—so no more of him here, henceforth, but good!

There is not so much color about as I had expected: and austerity rather than richness is the note of most of the exteriors.

I have not been allowed into the Uffizi yet, so to-day consoled myself with the Pitti. Titian's "Duke of Norfolk" is there, and I loved him, seeing a certain likeness there to somebody whom I—like. A photo of him will be coming to you. Also there is a very fine Lely-Vandyck of Charles I. and Henrietta Maria, a quite moral painting, making a triumphant assertion of that martyr's bad character. I imagine he got into heaven through having his head cut off and cast from him: otherwise all of him would have perished along with his mouth.

Somewhere too high up was hanging a ravishing Botticelli—a Madonna and Child bending over like a wind-blown tree to be kissed by St. John:—a composition that takes you up in its arms and rocks you as you look at it. Andrea del Sarto is to me only a big mediocrity: there is nothing here to touch his chortling child-Christ in our National Gallery.

At Pisa I slept in a mosquito-net, and felt like a bride at the altar under a tulle veil which was too large for her. Here, for lack of that luxury, being assured that there were no mosquitoes to be had, I have been sadly ravaged. The creatures pick out all foreigners, I think, and only when they have exhausted the supply do they pass on to the natives. Mrs. T—— left one foot unveiled when in Pisa, and only this morning did the irritation in the part bitten begin to come out.

I can now ask for a bath in Italian, and order the necessary things for myself in the hotel: also say " come in " and " thank you." But just the few days of that very German *table d'hôte* at Lucerne, where I talked gladly to polish myself up, have given my tongue a hybrid way of talking without thinking: and I say " *ja, ja,*" and " *nein,*" and " *der, die, das,*" as often as not before such Italian nouns as I have yet captured. To fall upon a chambermaid who knows French is like coming upon my native tongue suddenly.

Give me good news of your foot and all that is above it: I am so doubtful of its being really strong yet; and its willing spirits will overcome it some day and do it an injury, and hurt my feelings dreadfully at the same time.

Walk only on one leg whenever you think of me! I tell you truly I am wonderfully little lonely: and yet my thoughts are constantly away with you, wishing, wishing,—what no word on paper can ever carry to you. It shall be at our next meeting!—All yours.

## LETTER XXXII.

My Dearest: Florence is still eating up all my time and energies: I promised you there should be austerity and self-denial in the matter of letter-writing: and I know you are unselfish enough to expect even less than I send you.

Girls in the street address compliments to Arthur's complexion:—" beautiful brown boy " they call him: and he simmers over with vanity, and wishes he could show them his boating arms, brown up to the shoulder, as well. Have you noticed that combination in some of the dearest specimens of young English manhood,—great physical vanity and great mental modesty? and each as transparently sincere as the other.

The Bargello is an ideal museum for the storage of the best things out of the Middle Ages. It opens out of splendid courtyards and staircases, and ranges through rooms which have quite a feudal gloom about them; most of these are hung with bad late tapestries (too late at least for my taste), so that the gloom is welcome and charming, making even " Gobelins " quite bearable. I find quite a new man here to admire—Pollaiolo, both painter and sculptor, one of the school of "passionate anatomists," as I call them, about the time of Botticelli, I fancy. He has one bust of a young Florentine which equals Verocchio on the same ground, and charms me even more. Some of his subjects are done twice over, in paint and bronze: but he is more really a sculptor, I think, and merely paints his piece into a picture from its best point of view.

Verocchio's idea of David is charming: he is a saucy fellow who has gone in for it for the fun of the thing—knew he could bring down a hawk with his catapult, and therefore why not a Goliath also? If he failed, he need but cut and run, and everybody would laugh and call him plucky for doing even that much. So he does it, brings down his big game by good luck, and stands posing with a sort of irresistible stateliness to suit the result. He has a laugh something like "little Dick's," only more full of bubbles, and is saying to himself, "What a hero they all think me!" He is the merriest of sly-dog hypocrites, and has thin, wiry arms and a craney neck. He is a bit like Tom Sawyer in character, more ornate and dramatic than Huckleberry Finn, but quite as much a liar, given a good cause.

COURT YARD PALAZZO DEL BARGELLO.    P. 121.

Another thing that has seized me, more for its idea than actual carrying out, is an unnamed terra-cotta Madonna and Child. He is crushing himself up against her neck, open-mouthed and terrified, and she spreading long fingers all over his head and face. My notion of it is that it is the Godhead taking his first look at life from the human point of view; and he realizes himself " caught in his own trap," discovering it to be ever so much worse than it had seemed from an outside view. It is a fine modern *zeit-geist* piece of declamation to come out of the rather over-sweet della Robbia period of art.

There seems to have been a rage at one period for commissioning statues of David: so Donatello and others just turned to and did what they liked most in the way of budding youth, stuck a Goliath's head at its feet, and called it " David." Verocchio is the exception.

We are going to get outside Florence for a week or ten days; it is too hot to be borne at night after a day of tiring activity. So we go to the D——s' villa, which they offered us in their absence; it lies about four miles out, and is on much higher ground: address only your very immediately next letter there, or it may miss me.

There are hills out there with vineyards among them which draw me into wishing to be away from towns altogether. Much as I love what is to be found in this one, I think Heaven meant me to be "truly rural"; which all falls in, dearest, with what *I* mean to be! Beloved, how little I sometimes can say to you! Sometimes my heart can put only silence into the end of a letter; and with that I let this one go.— Yours, and so lovingly.

## LETTER XXXIII.

BELOVED: I had your last letter on Friday: all your letters have come in their right numbers. I have lost count of mine; but I think seven and two postcards is the total, which is the same as the numbers of clean and unclean beasts proportionately represented in the ark.

Up here we are out of the deadliness of the heat, and are thankful for it. Vineyards and olives brush the eyes between the hard, upright bars of the cypresses: and Florence below is like a hot bath which we dip into and come out again. At the Riccardi chapel I found Benozzo Gozzoli, not in crumbs, but perfectly preserved: a procession of early Florentine youths, turning into angels when they get to the bay of the window where the altar once stood. The more I see of them, the greater these early men seem to me: I shall be afraid to go to Venice soon; Titian will only half satisfy me, and Tintoretto, I know, will be actively annoying: I shall stay in my gondola, as your American lady did on her donkey after riding twenty miles to visit the ruins of—Carnac, was it not? It is well to have the courage of one's likings and dislikings, that is the only true culture (the state obtained by use of a "coulter" or cutter)—I cut many things severely which, no doubt, are good for other people.

Botticelli I was shy of, because of the craze about him among people who know nothing: he is far more wonderful than I had hoped, both at the Uffizi and the Academia: but he is quite pagan. I don't know why I say "but"; he is quite typical of the world's art-training: Christianity may get hold of the names and dictate the subjects, but the artist-breed carries a fairly level head through it all, and, like Pater's Mona Lisa, draws Christianity and Paganism into one: at least, wherever it reaches perfect expression it has done so. Some of the distinctly primitives are different; their works inclose a charm which is not artistic. Fra Angelico, after being a great disappointment to me in some of his large set pictures in the Academia and elsewhere, shows himself lovely in fresco (though I think the "crumb" element helps him). His great Crucifixion is big altogether, and has so permanent a force in its aloofness from mere drama and mere life. In San Marco, the cells of the monks are quite charming, a row of little square band-

boxes under a broad raftered corridor, and in
every cell is a beautiful little fresco for the monks
to live up to. But they no longer live there now:
all that part of San Marco has become a peep-
show.

I liked being in Savonarola's room, and was
more susceptible to the remains of his presence
than I have been to Michel Angelo or anyone
else's. Michel Angelo I feel most when he has
left a thing unfinished; then one can put one's
finger into the print of the chisel, and believe
anything of the beauty that might have come
out of the great stone chrysalis lying cased and
rough, waiting to be raised up to life.

Yesterday Arthur and I walked from here to
Fiesole, which we had neglected while in Florence—six miles going, and more like twelve coming back, all because of Arthur's absurd cross-
country instinct, which, after hours of river-
bends, bare mountain tracks, and tottering precipices, brought us out again half a mile nearer
Florence than when we started.

At Fiesole is the only church about here whose
interior architecture I have greatly admired, aus-
tere but at the same time gracious—like a Madonna of the best period of painting. We also
went to look at the Roman baths and theater:
the theater is charming enough, because it is still
there: but for the baths—oblongs of stone don't

interest me just because they are old.   All stone is old: and these didn't even hold water to give one the real look of the thing.   Too tired, and even more too lazy, to write other things, except love, most dear Beloved.

## LETTER XXXIV.

DEAREST: We were to have gone down with the rest into Florence yesterday: but soft miles of Italy gleamed too invitingly away on our right, and I saw Arthur's eyes hungry with the same far-away wish. So I said "Prato," and he ran up to the fattore's and secured a wondrous shandry-dan with just space enough between its horns to toss the two of us in the direction where we would go. Its gaunt framework was painted of a bright red, and our feet had only netting to rest on: so constructed, the creature was most vital and light of limb, taking every rut on the road with flea-like agility. Oh, but it was worth it!

We had a drive of fourteen miles through hills and villages, and castellated villas with gardens shut in by formidably high walls—always, a charm: a garden should always have something of the jealous seclusion of a harem. I am getting Italian landscape into my system, and enjoy it more and more.

Prato is a little cathedral town, very like the

narrow and tumble-down parts of Florence, only more so. The streets were a seething caldron of cattle-market when we entered, which made us feel like a tea-cup in a bull-ring (or is it thunderstorm?) as we drove through needle's-eye ways bristling with agitated horns.

The cathedral is little and good: damaged, of course, wherever the last three centuries have laid hands on it. At the corner of the west front is an out-door pulpit beautifully put on with a mushroom hood over its head. The main lines of the interior are finely severe, either quite round or quite flat, and proportions good always. An upholstered priest coming out to say mass is generally a sickening sight, so wicked and ugly in look and costume. The best-behaved people are the low-down beggars, who are most decoratively devotional.

We tried to model our exit on a brigand-beggar who came in to ask permission to murder one of his enemies. He got his request granted at one of the side-altars (some strictly local Madonna, I imagine), and his gratitude as he departed was quite touching. Having studiously copied his exit, we want to know whom we shall murder to pay ourselves for our trouble.

It amuses me to have my share of driving over these free and easy and very narrow highroads. But A. has to do the collision-shouting and the cries of " Via! "—the horse only smiles when he hears me do it.

Also did I tell you that on Saturday we two walked from here over to Fiesole—six miles there, and ten back: for why?—because we chose to go what Arthur calls " a bee-line across country," having thought we had sighted a route from the top of Fiesole. But in the valley we lost it, and after breaking our necks over precipices and our hearts down cul-de-sacs that led nowhere, and losing all the ways that were pointed out to us, for lack of a knowledge of the language, we came out again into view of Florence about half a mile nearer than when we started and proportionately far away from home. When he had got me thoroughly foot-sore, Arthur remarked complacently, " The right way to see a country is to lose yourself in it! " I didn't feel the truth of it then: but applied to other things I perceive its wisdom. Dear heart, where I have lost myself, what in all the world do I know so well as you?

Your most lost and loving.

## LETTER XXXV.

BELOVED: Rain swooped down on us from on high during the night, and the country is cut into islands: the river from a rocky wriggling stream has risen into a tawny, opaque torrent that roars with a voice a mile long and is become quite unfordable. The little mill-stream just below has broken its banks and poured itself away over the lower vineyards into the river; a lot of the vines look sadly upset, generally unhinged and unstrung, yet I am told the damage is really small. I hope so, for I enjoyed a real lash-out of weather, after the changelessness of the long heat.

I have been down in Florence beginning to make my farewells to the many things I have seen too little of. We start away for Venice about the end of the week. At the Uffizi I seem to have found out all my future favorites the first day, and very little new has come to me; but most of them go on growing. The Raphael lady is quite wonderful; I think she was in love with him, and her soul went into the painting though he himself did not care for her; and she looks at you and says, " See a miracle: he was able to paint this, and never knew that I loved him! " It is wonderful that; but I suppose it can be done,—a soul pass into a work and haunt it without its creator knowing anything about how it came there. Always when I come across anything like that which has something inner and rather mysterious, I tremble and want to get back to you. You are the touchstone by which I must test everything that is a little new and unfamiliar.

From now onwards, dearest, you must expect only cards for a time: it is not settled yet whether we stop at Padua on our way in or our way out. I am clamoring for Verona also; but that will be off our route, so Arthur and I may go there alone for a couple of greedy days, which I fear will only leave me dissatisfied and wishing I had had patience to depend on coming again—perhaps with you!

Uncle N. has written of your numerous visits to him, and I understand you have been very good in his direction. He does not speak of loneliness; and with Anna and her brood next week or now, he will be as happy as his temperament allows him to be when he has nothing to worry over.

I am proud to say I have gone brown without

freckles.  And are you really as cheerful as you write yourself to be?  Dearest and best, when is your holiday to begin; and is it to be with me?  Does anywhere on earth hold that happiness for us both in the near future?  I kiss you well, Beloved.

## LETTER XXXVI.

DEAREST: Venice is round me as I write!
Well, I will not waste my Baedeker knowledge
on you,—you too can get a copy; and it is not
the panoramic view of things you will be wanting from me: it is my own particular Venice I
am to find out and send you. So first of all
from the heart of it I send you mine: when I have
kissed you I will go on. My eyes have been
seeing so much that is new, I shall want a fresh
vocabulary for it all. But mainly I want to say,
let us be here again together quickly, before we
lose any more of our youth or our two-handed
hold on life. I get sort of breath thinking
of it!

So let it be here, Beloved, that some of our
soon-to-be happiness opens and shuts its eyes:
for truly Venice is a sleepy place. I am wanting, and taking, nine hours' sleep after all
I do!

Outside coming over the flats from Padua, she
looked something like a manufacturing town at

its ablutions,—a smoky chimney well to the forè: but get near to her and you find her standing on turquoise, her feet set about with jaspers, and with one of her eyes she ravishes you: and all her campanile are like the " thin flames " of "souls mounting up to God."

That is from without: within she becomes too sensuous and civic in her splendor to let me think much of souls. " Rest and be indolent " is the motto for the life she teaches. The architecture is the song of the lotos-eater built into stone— were I in a more florid mood I would have said " swan-song," for the whole stands finished with nothing more to be added: it has sung itself out: and if there is a moral to it all, no doubt it is in Ruskin, and I don't want to read it just now.

What I want is you close at hand looking up at all this beauty, and smiling when I smile, which is your way, as if you had no opinions of your own about anything in which you are not a professor. So you will write and agree that I am to have the pleasure of this return to look forward to? If I know that, I shall be so much more reconciled to all the joy of the things I am seeing now for the first time: and shall see so much better the second, Beloved, when your eyes are here helping me.

Here is love, dearest! help yourself to **just**

as much as you wish for; though all that I send is good for you! No letter from you since Florence, but I am neither sad nor anxious: only all the more your loving.

## LETTER XXXVII.

BELOVED: The weather is as gray as England to-day, and much rainier. To feel it on my cheeks and be back north with that and warmer things, I would go out in it in the face of protests, and had to go alone—not Arthur even being in the mood just then for a patriotic quest of the uncomfortable. I had myself oared into the lagoons across a racing current and a driving head-wind which made my gondolier bend like a distressed poplar over his oar; patience on a monument smiling at backsheesh—" all comes to him who knows."

Of course, for comfort and pleasure, and everything but economy, we have picked up a gondolier to pet: we making much of him, and he much out of us. He takes Arthur to a place where he can bathe—to use his own expression —" cleanly," that is to say, unconventionally; and this appropriately enough is on the borders of a land called " the Garden of Eden " (being named so after its owners). He—" Charon," I call him—is large and of ruddy countenance, and

talks English in blinkers—that is to say, gondola English—out of which he could not find
words to summon me a cab even if it were not
opposed to his interests. Still there are no cabs
to be called in Venice, and he is teaching us that
the shortest way is always by water. If Arthur
is not punctually in his gondola by 7 A. M., I
hear a call for the " Signore Inglese " go up to
his window; and it is hungry Charon waiting
to ferry him.

Yesterday your friend Mr. C—— called and
took me over to Murano in a beautiful pair-oared
boat that simply flew. There I saw a wonderful
apse filled with mosaic of dull gold, wherein is
set a blue-black figure of the Madonna, ten heads
high and ten centuries old, which almost made
me become a Mariolatrist on the spot. She
stands leaning up the bend with two pale hands
lifted in ghostly blessing. Underfoot the floor
is all mosaic, mountainous with age and earth-
quakes; the architecture classic in the grip of
Byzantine Christianity, which is like the spirit
of God moving on the face of the waters, or Eze-
kiel prophesying to the dry bones.

The Colleoni is quite as much more beautiful
in fact and seen full-size as I had hoped from
all smaller reproductions. A fine equestrian
figure always strikes one as enthroned, and not
merely riding; if I can't get that, I consider a

centaur the nobler creature with its human body set down into the socket of the brute, and all fire—a candle burning at both ends: which, in a way, is what the centaur means, I imagine?

Bellini goes on being wonderful, and for me beats Raphael's Blenheim Madonna period on its own ground. I hear now that the Raphael lady I raved over in Florence is no Raphael at all,— which accounts for it being so beautiful and interesting—to *me*, I hasten to add. Raphael's studied calmness, his soul of " invisible soap and imperceptible water," may charm some; me it only chills or leaves unmoved.

Is this more about art than you care to hear? I have nothing to say about myself, except that I am as happy as a cut-in-half thing can be. Is it any use sending kind messages to your mother? If so, my heart is full of them. Bless you, dearest, and good-night.

## LETTER XXXVIII.

DEAREST: St. Mark's inside is entirely different from anything I had imagined. I had expected a grove of pillars instead of these wonderful breadths of wall; and the marble overlay I had not understood at all till I saw it. My admiration mounts every time I enter: it has a different gloom from any I have ever been in, more joyous and satisfying, not in the least moody as our own Gothic seems sometimes to be; and saints instead of devils look at you solemn-eyed from every corner of shade.

A heavy rain turns the Piazza into a lake: this morning Arthur had to carry me across. Other foolish Englishwomen were shocked at such means, and paddled their own leaky canoes, or stood on the brink and looked miserable. The effect of rain-pool reflections on the inside of St. Mark's is noticeable, causing it to bloom unexpectedly into fresh subtleties and glories. The gold takes so sympathetically to any least tint of color that is in the air, and counts up the altar candles even unto its furthest recesses and cupolas.

I think before I leave Venice I shall find about ten Tintorettos which I really like. Best of all is that Bacchus and Ariadne in the Ducal Palace, of which you gave me the engraving. His " Marriage of St. Catherine," which is there also, has all Veronese's charm of color and what I call his " breeding "; and in the ceiling of the Council Chamber is one splendid figure of a sea-youth striding a dolphin.

Last evening we climbed the San Giorgio campanile for a sunset view of Venice; it is a much better point of view than the St. Mark's one, and we were lucky in our sunset. Venice again looked like a beautified factory town, blue and blue with smoke and evening mists. Down below in the church I met a delightful Capuchin priest who could talk French, and a poor, very young lay-brother who had the holy custody of the eyes heavily upon his conscience when I spoke to him. I was so sorry for him!

The Mother-Aunt is ill in bed; but as she is at the present moment receiving three visitors, you will understand about how ill. The fact is, she is worn to death with sight-seeing. I can't stop her; while she is on her legs it is her duty, and she will. The consequence is I get rushed through things I want to let soak into me, and have to go again. My only way of getting her to rest has been by deserting her; and then I come back and receive reproaches with a meek countenance.

Mr. C—— has been good to us and cordial, and brings his gondola often to our service. A gondola and pair has quite a different motion from a one-oared gondola; it is like riding a sea-horse instead of a sea-camel—almost exciting, only it is so soft in its prancings.

He took A. and myself into the procession which welcomed the crowned heads last Wednesday; the hurly-burly of it was splendid. We tore down the Grand Canal from end to end, almost cheek by jowl with the royalties; the M.-A. was quite jubilant when she heard we had had such " good places." Hundreds of gondolas swarmed round; many of them in the old Carpaccio rig-outs, very gorgeous though a little tawdry when taken out of the canvas. But the rush and the collisions, and the sound of many waters walloping under the bellies of the gondolas, and the blows of fighting oars—regular underwater wrestling matches—made it as vivid and amusing as a prolonged Oxford and Cambridge boat-race in fancy costume. Our gondoliers streamed with the exertion, and looked like men fighting a real battle, and yet enjoyed it thoroughly. Violent altercations with police-boats don't ruffle them at all; at one moment it looks daggers drawn; at the next it is shrugs and smiles. Often, from not knowing enough of Italian and Italian ways, I get hot all over when an ordinary discussion is going on, thinking that blows are about to be exchanged. The Mother-Aunt had hung a wonderful satin skirt out of window for decoration; and when she leaned over it in a bodice of the same color, it looked as if she were sitting with her legs out as well! I suppose it was this peculiar effect that, when the King and Queen came by earlier in the morning, won for her a special bow and smile.

I must hurry or I shall miss the post that I wish to catch. There seems little chance now of my getting you in Venice; but elsewhere perhaps you will drop to me out of the clouds.

Your own and most loving.

## LETTER XXXIX.

MY OWN, OWN BELOVED: Say that my being away does not seem too long? I have not had a letter yet, and that makes me somehow not anxious but compunctious; only writing to you of all I do helps to keep me in good conscience. Not the other foot gone to the mender's, I hope, with the same obstructive accompaniments as went to the setting-up again of the last? If I don't hear soon, you will have me dancing on wires, which cost as much by the word as a gondola by the hour.

Yesterday we went to see Carpaccio at his best in San Giorgio di Schiavone: two are St. George pictures, three St. Jeromes, and two of some other saint unknown to me. The St. Jerome series is really a homily on the love and pathos of animals. First is St. Jerome in his study with a sort of unclipped white poodle in the pictorial place of honor, all alone on a floor beautifully swept and garnished, looking up wistfully to his master busy at writing (a Benjy saying, "Come and take me for a walk, there's a

good saint! "). Scattered among the adornments
of the room are small bronzes of horses and, I
think, birds. So, of course, these being his
tastes, when St. Jerome goes into the wilderness,
a lion takes to him, and accompanies him when
he pays a call on the monks in a neighboring
monastery. Thereupon, holy men of little faith,
the entire fraternity take to their heels and rush
upstairs, the hindermost clinging to the skirts of
the formermost to be hauled the quicker out of
harm's way. And all the while the lion stands
incorrectly offering the left paw, and Jerome
with shrugs tries to explain that even the best
butter wouldn't melt in his dear lion's mouth.
After that comes the tragedy. St. Jerome lies
dying in excessive odor of sanctity, and all the
monks crowd round him with prayers and viati-
cums, and the ordinary stuffy pieties of a
" happy death," while Jerome wonders feebly
what it is he misses in all this to-do for which
he cares so little. And there, elbowed far out
into the cold, the lion lies and lifts his poor head
and howls because he knows his master is being
taken from him. Quite near to him, fastened to
a tree, a queer, nondescript, crocodile-shaped
dog runs out the length of its tether to comfort
the disconsolate beast: but *la bête humaine* has
got the whip-hand of the situation. In another
picture is a parrot that has just mimicked a dog,

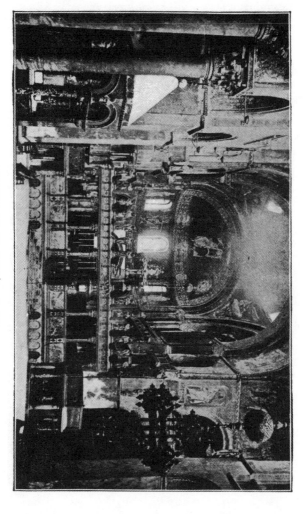

INTERIOR OF ST. MARK'S. P. 141.

or called " Carlo!" and then laughed: the dog turns his head away with a sleek, sheepish, shy look, exactly as a sensitive dog does when you make fun of him.

These are, perhaps, mere undercurrents of pictures which are quite glorious in color and design, but they help me to love Carpaccio to distraction; and when the others lose me, they hunt through all the Carpaccios in Venice till they find me!

Love me a little more if possible while I am so long absent from you! What I do and what I think go so much together now, that you will take what I write as the most of me that it is possible to cram in, coming back to you to share everything.

Under such an Italian sky as to-day how I would like to see your face! Here, dearest, among these palaces you would be in your peerage, for I think you have some southern blood in you.

Curious that, with all my fairness, somebody said to me to-day, " But you are not quite English, are you?" And I swore by the nine gods of my ancestry that I was nothing else. But the look is in us: my father had a foreign air, but made up for it by so violent a patriotism that Uncle N. used to call him " John Bull let loose."

My love to England. Is it showing much

autumn yet? My eyes long for green fields again. Since I have been in Italy I had not seen one until the other day from the top of St. Giorgio Maggiore, where one lies in hiding under the monastery walls.

All that I see now quickens me to fresh thoughts of you. Yet do not expect me to come back wiser: my last effort at wisdom was to fall in love with you, and there I stopped for good and all. There I am still, everything included: what do you want more? My letter and my heart both threaten to be over-weight, so no more of them this time. Most dearly do I love you.

## LETTER XL.

BELOVED: If two days slip by, I don't know where I am when I come to write; things get so crowded in such a short space of time. Where I left off I know not: I will begin where I am most awake—your letter which I have just received.

That is well, dearest, that is well indeed: a truce till February! And since the struggle then must needs be a sharp one—with only one end, as we know,—do not vex her now by any overt signs of preparation as if you assumed already that her final arguments were to be as so much chaff before the wind. You do not tell me *what* she argues, and I do not ask. She does not say I shall not love you enough!

To answer businesslike to your questions first: with your forgiveness we stay here till the 25th, and get back to England with the last of the month. Does that seem a very cruel, far-off date? Others have the wish to stay even longer, and it would be no fairness to hurry them beyond a certain degree of reasonableness with my

particular reason for impatience, seeing, more-
over, that in your love I have every help for remaining patient. It is too much to hope, I suppose, that the " truce " sets you free now, and that
you could meet us here after all, and prolong our
stay indefinitely? I know one besides myself
who would be glad, and would welcome an outside excuse dearly.

For, oh, the funniness of near and dear things!
Arthur's heart is laid up with a small love affair,
and it is the comicalest of internal maladies. He
is screwing up courage to tell me all about it,
and I write in haste before my mouth is sealed
by his confidences. I fancy I know the party,
an energetic little mortal whom we met at Lucerne, where Arthur lingered while we came on
to Florence. She talked vaguely of being in
Venice some time this autumn; and the vague-
ness continues. Arthur, in consequence, roams
round disconsolately with no interest but in hotel
books. And for fear lest we should gird up his
loins and drag him away with us out of Para-
disal possibilities, he is forever praising Venice
as a resting-place, and saying he wants to be nowhere else. The bathing just keeps him alive;
but when put to it to explain what charms him
since pictures do not, and architecture only
slightly, he says in exemplary brotherly fashion
that he likes to see me completing my educa-

tion and enthusiasms,—and does not realize with
how foreign an air that explanation sits upon his
shoulders.

I saw to-day a remnant of your patron saint,
and for your sake transferred a kiss to it, Italian
fashion, with my thumb and the sign of the cross.
I hope it will do you good. Also, I have been
up among the galleries of St. Mark's, and about
the roof and the west front where somebody or
another painted his picture of the bronze horses.
The pigeons get to recognize people person-
ally, and grow more intimate every time we
come. I even conceive they make favorites, for
I had three pecking food out of my mouth to-
day and refusing to take it in any other fashion,
and they coo and say thank you before and after
every seed they take or spill. They are quite
the pleasantest of all the Italian beggars—and
the cleanest.

Your friend pressed us in to tea yesterday: I
think less for the sake of giving us tea than that
we should see his palace, or rather his first floor,
in which alone he seems to lose himself. I have
no idea for measurements, but I imagine his big
sala is about eighty feet long and perhaps
twenty-five feet across, with a flat-beamed roof,
windows at each end, and portières along the
walls of old blue Venetian linen: a place in which
it seems one could only live and think nobly.

His face seems to respond to its teachings. What more might not an environment like that bring out in you? Come and let me see! I have hopes springing as I think of things that you may be coming after all; and that that is what lay concealed under the gayety of your last paragraph. Then I am more blessed even than I knew. What, you are coming? So well I do love you, my Beloved!

## LETTER XLI.

DEAREST: This letter will travel with me: we leave to-day. Our movements are to be too restless and uncomfortable for the next few days for me to have a chance of quiet seeing or quiet writing anywhere. At Riva we shall rest, I hope.

Yesterday a storm began coming over towards evening, and I thought to myself that if it passed in time there should be a splendid sunset of smolder and glitter to be seen from the Campanile, and perhaps by good chance a rainbow.

I went alone: when I got to the top the rain was pelting hard; so there I stayed happily weather-bound for an hour looking over Venice " silvered with slants of rain," and watching umbrellas scuttering below with toes beneath them. The golden smolder was very slow in coming: it lay over the mainland and came creeping along the railway track. Then came the glitter and the sun, and I turned round and found my rainbow. But it wasn't a bow, it was a circle: the

Campanile stood up as it were a spoke in the middle,—the lower curve of the rainbow lay on the ground of the Piazzetta, cut off sharp by the shadow of the Campanile. It was worth waiting an hour to see. The islands shone mellow and bright in the clearance with the storm going off black behind them. Good-by, Venice!

Verona began by seeming dull to me; but it improves and unfolds beautiful corners of itself to be looked at: only I am given so little time. The Tombs of the Della Scalas and the Renaissance façade of the Consiglio are what chiefly delight me. I had some quiet hours in the Museo, where I fell in love with a little picture by an unknown painter, of Orpheus charming the beasts in a wandering green landscape, with a dance of fauns in the distance, and here and there Eurydice running;—and Orpheus in Hades, and the Thracian women killing him, and a crocodile fishing out his head, and mermaids and ducks sitting above their reflections reflecting.

Also there is one beautiful Tobias and the Angel there by a painter whose name I most ungratefully forget. I saw a man yesterday carrying fishes in the market, each strung through the gills on a twig of myrtle: that is how Tobias ought to carry his fish: when a native custom suggests old paintings, how charming it always is!

RIVA.

We have just got here from Verona. In the matter of the garden at least it is a Paradise of a place. A great sill of honeysuckle leans out from my window: beyond is a court grown round with creepers, and beyond that the garden—such a garden! The first thing one sees is an arcade of vines upon stone pillars, between which peep stacks of roses, going off a little from their glory now, and right away stretches an alley of green, that shows at the end, a furlong off, the blue glitter of water. It is a beautifully wild garden: grass and vegetables and trees and roses all grow in a jungle together. There are little groves of bamboo and chestnut and willow; and a runnel of water is somewhere—I can hear it. It suggests rest, which I want; and so, for all its difference, suggests you, whom also I want,—more, I own it now, than I have said! But that went without saying, Beloved, as it always must if it is to be the truth and nothing short of the truth.

While this has been waiting to go, your letter has been put into my hands. I am too happy to say words about it, and can afford now to let this go as it is. The little time of waiting for you will be perfect happiness now; and your coming seems to color all that is behind as well. I have had a good time indeed, and was only wearying with the plethora of my enjoyment: but the better time has been kept till now. We shall be together day after day and all day long for at least a month, I hope: a joy that has never happened to us yet.

Never mind about the lost letter now, dearest, dearest: Venice was a little empty just one week because of it. I still hope it will come; but what matter?—I know *you* will. All my heart waits for you.—Your most glad and most loving.

## LETTER XLII.

Dearest: I saw an old woman riding a horse astride: and I was convinced on the spot that this is the rightest way of riding, and that the side-saddle was a foolish and affected invention. The horse was fine, and so was the young man leading it: the old woman was upright and stately, with a wide hat and full petticoats like a Maximilian soldier.

This was at Bozen, where we stayed for two nights, and from which I have brought a cold with me: it seems such an English thing to have, that I feel quite at home in the discomfort of it. It had been such wonderful weather that we were sitting out of doors every evening up to 9.30 p. m. without wraps, and on our heads only our "widows' caps." (The M.-A. persists in a style which suggests that Uncle N. has gone to a better world.) Mine was too flimsy a work of fiction, and a day before I had been for a climb and got wet through, so a chill laid its benediction on my head, and here I am,—not seriously incommoded by the malady, but by the remedy, which is the M.-A. full of kind quackings and fierce tyranny if I do but put my head out of window to admire the view, whose best is a little round the corner.

I had no idea Innsbruck was so high up among the mountains: snows are on the peaks all around. Behind the house-tops, so close and near, lies a quarter circle of white crests. You are told that in winter creatures come down and look in at the windows: sometimes they are called wolves, sometimes bears—any way the feeling is mediæval.

Hereabouts the wayside shrines nearly always contain a crucifix, whereas in Italy that was rare —the Virgin and Child being the most common. I remarked on this, which I suppose gave rise to a subsequent observation of the M.-A.'s: " I think the Tyrolese are a *good* people: they are not given over to Mariolatry like those poor priest-ridden Italians." I think, however, that they merely have that fundamental grace, religious simplicity, worshiping—just what they can get, for yesterday I saw two dear old bodies going round and telling their beads before the bronze statues of the Maximilian tomb—King Arthur, Charles the Bold, etc. I suppose, by mere association, a statue helps them to pray.

The national costume does look so nice, though not exactly beautiful. I like the flat, black hats with long streamers behind and a gold tassel, and the spacious apron. Blue satin is a favorite style, always silk or satin for Sunday best: one I saw of pearl-white brocade.

Since we came north we have had lovely weather, except the one day of which I am still the filterings: and morning along the Brenner Pass was perfect. I think the mountains look most beautiful quite early, at sunrise, when they are all pearly and mysterious.

We go on to Zurich on Thursday, and then, Beloved, and then!—so this must be my last letter, since I shall have nowhere to write to with you rushing all across Europe and resting nowhere because of my impatience to have you. The Mother-Aunt concedes a whole month, but Arthur will have to leave earlier for the beginning of term. How little my two dearest men have yet seen of each other! Barely a week lies between us: this will scarcely catch you. Dearest of dearests, my heart waits on yours.

## LETTER XLIII.

My Dearest: See what an effect your "gallous young hound" episode has had on me. I send it back to you roughtly done into rhyme. I don't know whether it will carry; for, outside your telling of it, "Johnnie Kigarrow" is not a name of heroic sound. What touches me as so strangely complete about it is that you should have got that impression and momentary romantic delusion as a child, and now hear, years after, of his disappearing out of life thus fittingly and mysteriously, so that his name will fix its legend to the countryside for many a long day. I would like to go there some day with you, and standing on Twloch Hill imagine all the country round as the burial-place of the strong man on whose knees my beloved used to play when a child.

It must have been soon after this that your brother died: truly, dearest, from now, and strangely, this Johnnie Kigarrow will seem more to me than him; touching a more heroic strain of idea, and stiffening fibers in your nature that brotherhood, as a rule, has no bearing on.

A short letter to-day, Beloved, because what goes with it is so long. This is the first time I have come before your eyes as anything but a letter-writer, and I am doubtful whether you will care to have so much all about yourself. Yet for that very reason think how much I loved doing it! I am jealous of those days before I knew you, and want to have all their wild-honey flavor for myself. Do remember more, and tell me! Dearest heart, it was to me you were coming through all your scampers and ramblings; no wonder, with that unknown good running parallel, that my childhood was a happy one. May long life bless you, Beloved!

*(Inclosure.)*

My brother and I were down in Wales,
And listened by night to the Welshman's tales;
He was eleven and I was ten.
We sat on the knees of the farmer's men
After the whole day's work was done:
And I was friends with the farmer's son.
His hands were rough as his arms were strong,
His mouth was merry and loud for song;
Each night when set by the ingle-wall
He was the merriest man of them all.
I would catch at his beard and say
All the things I had done in the day—
Tumbled bowlders over the force,
Swum in the river and fired the gorse—
" Half the side of the hill ! " quoth I :—
" Ah ! " cried he, " and didn't you die ?"

" Chut! " said he, " but the squeak was narrow !
Didn't you meet with Johnnie Kigarrow ? "
" No ! " said I, " and who will he be ?
And what will be Johnnie Kigarrow to me ? "
The farmer's son said under his breath,
" Johnnie Kigarrow may be your death !
Listen you here, and keep you still—
Johnnie Kigarrow bides under the hill ;
Twloch barrow stands over his head;
He shallows the river to make his bed ;
Bowlders roll when he stirs a limb ;
And the gorse on the hills belongs to him !
And if so be one fires his gorse,
He's out of his bed, and he mounts his horse.
Off he sets : with the first long stride
He is halfway over the mountain side :
 With his second stride he has crossed the barrow,
And he has you fast, has Johnnie Kigarrow ! "

Half I laughed and half I feared ;
I clutched and tugged at the strong man's beard,
And bragged as brave as a boy could be—
" So ? but, you see, he didn't catch me ! "

Fear caught hold of me : what had I done ?
High as the roof rose the farmer's son :
How the sight of him froze my marrow !
" I," he cried, " am Johnnie Kigarrow ! "

Well, you wonder, what was the end ?
Never forget ;—he had called me " friend " !
Mighty of limb, and hard, and brown ;
Quickly he laughed and set me down.
" Heh ! " said he, " but the squeak was narrow,
Not to be caught by Johnnie Kigarrow ! "

"INSBRUCK WAS SO HIGH UP AMONG THE MOUNTAINS." P. 158.

Now, I hear, after years gone by,
Nobody knows how he came to die.
He strode out one night of storm :
" Get you to bed, and keep you warm ! "
Out into darkness so went he :
Nobody knows where his bones may be.

Only I think—if his tongue let go
Truth that once,—how perhaps *I* know.
Twloch river, and Twloch barrow,
Do you cover my Johnnie Kigarrow ?

## LETTER XLIV.

DEAREST: I have been doing something so wise and foolish: mentally wise, I mean, and physically foolish. Do you guess?—Disobeying your parting injunction, and sitting up to see eclipses.

It was such a luxury to do as I was *not* told just for once; to feel there was an independent me still capable of asserting itself. My belief is that, waking, you hold me subjugated: but, once your godhead has put on its spiritual nightcap, and begun nodding, your mesmeric influence relaxes. Up starts resolution and independence, and I breathe desolately for a time, feeling myself once more a free woman.

'Twas a tremulous experience, Beloved; but I loved it all the more for that. How we love playing at grief and death—the two things that must come—before it is their due time! I took a look at my world for three most mortal hours last night, trying to see you *out* of it. And oh, how close it kept bringing me! I almost heard

you breathe, and was forever wondering—Can
we ever be nearer, or love each other more than
we do? For *that* we should each want a sixth
sense, and a second soul: and it would still be
only the same spread out over larger territory.
I prefer to keep it nesting close in its present
limitations, where it feels like a " growing pain ";
children have it in their legs, we in our
hearts.

I am growing sleepy as I write, and feel I am
sending you a dull letter,—my penalty for doing
as you forbade.

I sat up from half-past one to a quarter to five
to see our shadow go over heaven. I didn't see
much, the sky was too piebald: but I was not
disappointed, as I had never watched the darkness into dawn like that before: and it was interesting to hear all the persons awaking:—cocks
at half-past four, frogs immediately after, then
pheasants and various others following. I was
cuddled close up against my window, throned
in a big arm-chair with many pillows, a spirit-
lamp, cocoa, bread and butter, and buns; so I
fared well. Just after the pheasants and the first
querulous fidgetings of hungry blackbirds comes
a soft pattering along the path below: and Benjy,
secretive and important, is fussing his way to
the shrubbery, when instinct or real sentiment
prompts him to look up at my window; he gives

a whimper and a wag, and goes on. I try to
persuade myself that he didn't see me, and that
he does this, other mornings, when I am not thus
perversely bolstered up in rebellion, and peering
through blinds at wrong hours. Isn't there
something pathetic in the very idea that a dog
may have a behind-your-back attachment of that
sort?—that every morning he looks up at an un-
responsive blank, and wags, and goes by?

I heard him very happy in the shrubs a moment after: he and a pheasant, I fancy, disputing
over a question of boundaries. And he comes
in for breakfast, three hours later, looking posi-
tively *fresh*, and wants to know why I am yawn-
ing.

Most mornings he brings your letter up to my
room in his mouth. It is old Nan-nan's joke:
she only sends up *yours* so, and pretends it is
Benjy's own clever selection. I pretend that,
too, to him; and he thinks he is doing something
wonderful. The other morning I was—well,
Benjy hears splashing: and tires of waiting—or
his mouth waters. An extra can of hot water
happens to stand at the door; and therein he de-
posits his treasure (mine, I mean), and retires
saying nothing. The consequence is, when I
open three minutes after his scratch, I find you
all ungummed and swimming, your beautiful
handwriting bleared and smeared, so that no eye

but mine could have read it. Benjy's shame
when I showed him what he had done was wonderful.

How it rejoices me to write quite foolish
things to you!—that I *can* helps to explain a
great deal in the up-above order of things, which
I never took in when I was merely young and
frivolous. One must have touched a grave side
of life before one can take in that Heaven is not
opposed to laughter.

My eye has just caught back at what I have
written; and the " little death " runs through me,
just because I wrote " grave side." It shouldn't,
but loving has made me superstitious: the happiness seems too great; how can it go on? I keep
thinking—this is not life: you are too much for
me, my dearest!

Oh, my Beloved, come quickly to meet me
to-day: this morning! Ride over; I am willing
it. My own dearest, you must come. If you
don't, what shall I believe? That Love cannot
outdo space: that when you are away I cannot
reach you by willing. But I can: come to me!
You shall see my arms open to you as
never before. What is it?—you must be coming. I have more love in me after all than I
knew.

Ah, I know: I wrote " grave side," and all my
heart is in arms against the treason. With us

it is not " till death us do part ": we leap it alto-gether, and are clasped on the other side.

My dear, my dear, I lay my head down on your heart: I love you!   I post this to show how certain I am.   At twelve to-day I shall see you.

## LETTER XLV.

BELOVED: I look at this ridiculous little nib now, running like a plow along the furrows! What can the poor thing do? Bury its poor black, blunt little nose in the English language in order to tell you, in all sorts of roundabout ways, what you know already as well as I do. And yet, though that is all it can do, you complain of not having had a letter! Not had a letter? Beloved, there are half a hundred I have not had from you! Do you suppose you have ever, any one week in your life, sent me as many as I wanted?

Now, for once, I did hold off and didn't write to you: because there was something in your last I couldn't give any answer to, and I hoped you would come yourself before I need. Then I hoped silence would bring you: and now—no! —instead of your dear peace-giving face I get this complaint!

Ah, Beloved, have you in reality any complaint, or sorrow that I can set at rest? Or has that little, little silence made you anxious? I

do come to think so, for you never flourish your
words about as I do: so, believing that, I would
like to write again differently; only it is truer to
let what I have written stand, and make amends
for it in all haste.   I love you so infinitely well,
how could even a year's silence give you any
doubt or anxiety, so long as you knew I was
not ill?

   " Should one not make great concessions to
great grief even when it is unreasonable?"    I
cannot answer, dearest: I am in the dark.   Great
grief cannot be great without reasons: it should
give them, and you should judge by them:—you,
not I.   I imagine you have again been face to
face with fierce, unexplained opposition.   Dearest, if it would give you happiness, I would say,
make five, ten, twenty years' "concession," as
you call it.   But the only time you ever spoke
to me clearly about your mother's mind toward
me, you said she wanted an absolute surrender
from you, not covered only by her lifetime.
Then though I pitied her, I had to smile.   A
twenty years' concession even would not give
rest to her perturbed spirit.   I pray truly—having so much reason for your sake to pray it—
" God rest her soul! and give her a saner mind
toward both of us."

   Why has this come about at all?   It is not
February yet: and *our* plans have been putting

forth no buds before their time. When the day comes, and you have said the inevitable word, I think more calm will follow than you expect. *You*, dearest, I do understand: and the instinct of tenderness you have toward a claim which yet fills you with the sense of its injustice. I know that you can laugh at her threat to make you poor; but not at hurting her affections. Did your asking for an "answer" mean that I was to write so openly? Bless you, my own dearest.

## LETTER XLVI.

DEAREST: To-day I came upon a strange spectacle: poor old Nan-nan weeping for wounded pride in me. I found her stitching at raiment of needlework that is to be mine (piles of it have been through her fingers since the word first went out; for her love asserts that I am to go all home-made from my old home to my new one—wherever that may be!). And she was weeping because, as I slowly got to understand, from one particular quarter too little attention had been paid to me:—the kow-tow of a ceremonious reception into my new status had not been deep enough to make amends to her heart for its partial loss of me.

Her deferential recognition of the change which is coming is pathetic and full of etiquette; it is at once so jealous and so unselfish. Because her sense of the proprieties will not allow her to do so much longer, she comes up to my room and makes opportunity to scold me over quite slight things:—and there I am, meeker under

her than I would be to any relative. So to-day
I had to bear a statement of your mother's in-
firmities rigorously outlined in a way I could
only pretend to be deaf to until she had done.
Then I said, "Nan-nan, go and say your
prayers!" And as she stuck her heels down and
refused to go, there I left the poor thing, not to
prayer, I fear, but to desolate weeping, in which
love and pride will get more firmly entangled
together than ever.

I know when I go up to my room next I shall
find fresh flowers put upon my table: but the
grievous old dear will be carrying a sore heart
that I cannot comfort by any words. I cannot convince her that I am not hiding in myself any wounds such as she feels on my
behalf.

I write this, dearest, as an indirect answer to
yours,—which is but Nan-nan's woe writ large.
If I could persuade your two dear and very different heads how very slightly wounded I am by
a thing which a little waiting will bring right,
I could give it even less thought than I do. Are
you keeping the truce in spirit when you disturb
yourself like this? Trust me, Beloved, always to
be candid: I will complain to you when I feel in
need of comfort. Be comforted yourself, meanwhile, and don't shape ghosts of grief which
never do a goose-step over me! Ah well, well,

if there is a way to love you better than I do now, only show it me! Meantime, think of me as your most contented and happy-go-loving.

## LETTER XLVII.

DEAREST: I am haunted by a line of quotation, and cannot think where it comes from:

"Now sets the year in roaring gray."

Can you help me to what follows? If it is a true poem it ought now to be able to sing itself to me at large from an outer world which at this moment is all gray and roaring. To-day the year is bowing itself out tempestuously, as if angry at having to go. Dear golden year! I am sorry to see its face so changed and withering: it has held so much for us both. Yet I am feeling vigorous and quite like spring. All the seasons have their marches, with buffetings and border-forays: this is an autumn march-wind; before long I shall be out into it, and up the hill to look over at your territory and you being swept and garnished for the seven devils of winter.

"Roaring gray" suggests Tennyson, whom I do very much associate with this sort of weather, not so much because of passages in "Maud" and

" In Memoriam " as because I once went over
to Swainston, on a day such as this when rooks
and leaves alike hung helpless in the wind; and
heard there the story of how Tennyson, coming
over for his friend's funeral, would not go into
the house, but asked for one of Sir John's old
hats, and with that on his head sat in the garden
and wrote almost the best of his small lyrics:

> " Nightingales warbled without,
>    Within was weeping for thee."

The " old hat " was mentioned as something hu-
morous: yet an old glove is the most accepted
symbol of faithful absence: and why should head
rank lower than hand?   What creatures of convention we are!

There is an old notion, quite likely to be true,
that a nightcap carries in it the dreams of its
first owner, or that anything laid over a sleeper's
head will bring away the dream.   One of the
stories which used to put a lump in my throat
as a child was of an old backwoodsman who by
that means found out that his dog stole hams
from the storeroom.   The dog was given away
in disgrace, and came to England to die of a
broken heart at the sight of a cargo of hams,
which, at their unpacking, seemed like a monstrous day of judgment—the bones of his mis-
deeds rising again reclothed with flesh to re-

proach him with the thing he had never forgotten.

I wonder how long it was before I left off definitely choosing out a story for the pleasure of
making myself cry! When one begins to avoid
that luxury of the fledgling emotions, the first
leaf of youth is flown.

To-day I look almost jovially at the decay of
the best year I have ever lived through, and am
your very middle-aged faithful and true.

## LETTER XLVIII.

DEAREST: If anybody has been "calling me names" that are not mine, they do me a fine injury, and you did well to purge the text of their abuse. I agree with no authority, however immortal, which inquires "What's in a name?" expecting the answer to be a snap of the fingers. I answer with a snap of temper that the blood, boots, and bones of my ancestors are in mine! Do you suppose I could have been the same woman had such names as Amelia or Bella or Cinderella been clinging leechlike to my consciousness through all the years of my training? Why, there are names I can think of which would have made me break down into side-ringlets had I been forced to wear them audibly.

The effect is not so absolute when it is a second name that can be tucked away if unpresentable, but even then it is a misfortune. There is C——, now, who won't marry, I believe, chiefly because of the insane "Annie" with which she was smitten at the baptismal font by an afterthought. She regards it as a taint in her constitution which orders her to a lonely life lest

THE ALBERT MEMORIAL.   P. 179.

worse might follow. And apply the considera-
tion more publicly: do you imagine the Prince of
Wales will be the same sort of king if, when he
comes to the throne, he calls himself King Albert
Edward in florid Continental fashion, instead of
" Edward the Seventh," with a right hope that
an Edward the Eighth may follow after him, to
make a neck-and-neck race of it with the Hen-
ries? I don't know anything that would do more
to knit up the English constitution: but whenever
I pass the Albert Memorial I tremble lest filial
piety will not allow the thing to be done.

Now of all this I had an instance in the village
the day before yesterday. At the corner house by
the post-office, as I went by, a bird opened his bill
and sang a note, and down, down, down, down
he went over a golden scale: pitched afresh, and
dropped down another; and then up, up, up, over
the range of both. Then he flung back his
shaggy head and laughed. " In all my father's
realm there are no such bells as these!" It was
the laughing jackass. " Who gave you your
name?" " My godfathers and my godmothers in
my baptism." Well, *his* will have *that* to answer
for, however safely for the rest he may have es-
chewed the world, the flesh, and the devil. Poor
bird, to be set to sing to us under such a burden:
—of which, unconscious failure, he knows nothing.

Here I have remembered for you a bit of a poem that took hold of me some while ago and touched on the same unkindness: only here the flower is conscious of the wrong done to it, and looks forward to a day of juster judgment:—

> " What have I done ?—Man came
>     (There's nothing that sticks like dirt),
>     Looked at me with eyes of blame,
>     And called me ' Squinancy-wort !'
>     What have I done ?   I linger
>     (I cannot say that I live)
>     In the happy lands of my birth ;
>     Passers-by point with the finger :
>     For me the light of the sun
>     Is darkened.   Oh, what would I give
>     To creep away, and hide my shame in the earth !
>     What have I done ?
>     Yet there is hope.   I have seen
>     Many changes since I began.
>     The web-footed beasts have been
>     (Dear beasts!)—and gone, being part of some wider plan.
>     Perhaps in His infinite mercy God will remove this
>         man ! "

Now I am on sentiment and unjust judgments: here is another instance, where evidently in life I did not love well enough a character nobler than this capering and accommodating boy Benjy, who toadies to all my moods.  Calling at the lower farm, I missed him whom I used to nickname " Manger," because his dog-jaws always refused to smile on me.   His old mistress gave me a pathetic account of his last days. It was the muzzling order that broke his poor old heart. He took it as an accusation on a point where, though of a melancholy disposition, his reputation had been spotless. He never lifted his head nor smiled again. And not all his mistress' love could explain to him that he was not in fault. She wept as she told it me.

Good-by, dearest, and for this letter so full of such little worth call me what names you like; and I will go to Jemima, Keziah, and Kerenhappuch for the patience in which they must have taken after their father when he so named them, I suppose for a discipline.

My Beloved, let my heart come where it wants to be. Twilight has been on me to-day, I don't know why; and I have not written it off as I hoped to do.—All yours and nothing left.

## LETTER XLIX.

DEAREST: I suppose your mother's continued absence, and her unexplanation of her further stay, must be taken for unyielding disapproval, and tells us what to expect of February. It is not a cordial form of " truce ": but since it lets me see just twice as much of you as I should otherwise, I will not complain so long as it does not make you unhappy. You write to her often and kindly, do you not?

Well, if this last letter of hers frees you sufficiently, it is quite settled at this end that you are to be with us for Christmas:—read into that the warmest corners of a heart already fully occupied. I do not think of it too much, till I am assured it is to be.

Did you go over to Pembury for the day? Your letter does not say anything: but your letters have a wonderful way with them of leaving out things of outside importance. I shall hear from the rattle of returning fire-engines some day that Hatterling has been burned down: and you will arrive cool the next day and say, "Oh yes, it is so!"

I am sure you have been right to secure this pledge of independence to yourself: but it hurts me to think what a deadly offense it may be both to her tenderness for you and her pride and stern love of power. To realize suddenly that Hatterling does not mean to you so much as the power to be your own master and happy in your own way, which is altogether opposite to *her* way, will be so much of a blow that at first you will be able to do nothing to soften it.

February fill-dyke is likely to be true to its name, this coming one, in all that concerns us and our fortunes. Meanwhile, if at Pembury you brought things any nearer settlement, and are not coming so soon as to-morrow, let me know: for some things of "outside importance" do affect me unfavorably while in suspense. I have not your serene determination to abide the workings of Kismet when once all that can be done is done.

The sun sets now, when it does so visibly, just where Pembury *is*. I take it as an omen. In your diary to-morrow you may write down in the business column that you have had a business letter from *me,* or as near to one as I can go:— chiefly for that it requires an answer on this matter of "outside importance," which otherwise you will altogether leave out. But you will do better still to come. My whole heart goes out to fetch you: my dearest dear, ever your own.

## LETTER L.

BELOVED: No, not Browning but Tennyson was in my thoughts at our last ride together: and I found myself shy, as I have been for a long time wishing to say things I could not. What has never entered your head to ask becomes difficult when I wish to get it spoken. So I bring Tennyson to tell you what I mean:—

" Dosn't thou 'ear my 'erse's legs, as they canters awaäy?
Proputty, proputty, proputty—that's what I 'ears 'em saäy."

The tune of this kept me silent all the while we galloped: this and Pembury, a name that glows to me now like the New Jerusalem.

And do you understand, Beloved? or must I say more? My freedom has made its nest under my uncle's roof: but I *am* a quite independent person in other ways besides character.

Well, Pembury was settled on your own initiative: and I looked on proud and glad. Now I have my own little word to add, merely a tail that wags and makes merry over a thing decided and done. Do you forgive me for this: and for

the greater offense of being quite shy at having
to write it?

My Aunt thanks you for the game: for my
part I cannot own that it will taste sweeter to me
for being your own shooting. And please, whatever else you do big and grand and dangerous,
respect my superstitions and don't shoot any
larks this winter. In the spring I would like to
think that here or there an extra lark bubbles
over because I and my whims find occasional favor in your sight. When I ask great favors you
always grant them; and so, Ahasuerus, grant this
little one to your beautifully loving.

Give me the credit of being conscious of it,
Beloved: postscripts I never *do* write. I am glad
you noticed it. If I find anything left out I start
another letter: *this* is that other letter: it goes
into the same envelope merely for company, and
signs itself yours in all state.

"OUR POSTMAN IS A LOVELY SIGHT." P. 180.

## LETTER LI.

DEAREST: It was so nice and comedy to see the Mother-Aunt this morning importantly opening a letter from you all to herself with the pleasure quite unmixed by any inclosure for me, or any other letter in the house *to* me so far as she was aware. I listened to you with new ears, discovering that you write quite beautifully in the style which I never get from you. Don't, because I admire you in your more formal form, alter in your style to me. I prefer you much, for my own part, formless: and feel nearer to your heart in an unfinished sentence than in one that is perfectly balanced. Still I want you to know that your cordial warmed her dear old heart and makes her not think now that she has let me see too much of you. She was just beginning to worry herself jealously into that belief the last two days: and Arthur's taking to you helped to the same end. Very well; I seem to understand everybody's oddities now,—having made a complete study of yours.

Best Beloved, I have your little letter lying

close, and feel dumb when I try to answer. You with your few words make me feel a small thing with all my unpenned rabble about me. Only you do know so very well that I love you better than I can ever write. This is my first letter of the new year: will our letter-writing go on all this year, or will it, as we dearly dream, die a divine death somewhere before autumn?

In any case, I am, dearest, your most happy and loving.

## LETTER LII.

My Dearest: Arthur and the friend went off together yesterday. I am glad the latter stayed just long enough after you left for me to have leisure to find him out human. Here is the whole story: he came and unbosomed to me three days ago: and he said nothing about not telling, so I tell you. As water goes from a duck's back, so go all things worth hearing from me to you.

Arthur had said to him, " Come down for a week," and he had answered, " Can't, because of clothes!" explaining that beyond evening-dress he had only those he stood in. " Well," said Arthur, " stand in them, then; you look all right." " The question is," said his friend, " can I sit down?" However, he came; and was appalled to find that a man unpacked his trunk, and would in all probability be carrying away his clothes each night to brush them. He, conscious of interiors, a lining hanging in rags, and even a patching somewhere, had not the heart to let his one and only day-jacket go down to the servants' hall to be sniffed over: and so every evening when he dressed for dinner he hid his jacket laboriously under the permanent layers of a linen wardrobe which stood in his room.

I had all this in the frankest manner from him in the hour when he became human: and my fancy fired at the vision. Graves with a fierce eye set on duty probing hither and thither in search after the missing coat; and each night the search becoming more strenuous and the mystery more baffling than ever. It had a funny likeness to the Jack Raikes episode in " Evan Harrington," and pleased me the more thus cropping up in real life.

Well, I demanded there and then to be shown the subject of so much romance and adventure: and had the satisfaction of mending it, he sitting by in his shirt-sleeves the while, and watching delighted and without craven apologies.

I notice it is not his own set he is ashamed of, but only the moneyed, high-sniffing servant-class who have no understanding for honorable poverty: and to be misunderstood pricks him in the thinnest of thin places.

He told me also that he brought only three white ties to last him for seven days: and that Graves placed them out in order of freshness and cleanliness night after night:—first three new ones consecutively, then three once worn. After that, on the seventh day, Graves resigned all further responsibility, and laid out all three of them for him to choose from. On the last three days of his stay he did me the honor to leave his coat out, declaring that my mendings had made it presentable before an emperor. Out of this dates the whole of his character, and I understand, what I did not, why Arthur and he get on together.

Now the house is empty, and your comings will be—I cannot say more welcome: but there will be more room for them to be after my own heart.

Heaven be over us both. Faithfully your most loving.

## LETTER LIII.

BELOVED: I wish you could have been with me
to look out into this garden last night when the
spirit moved me there. I had started for bed,
but became sensitive of something outside not nor-
mal. Whether my ear missed the usual echoes
and so guessed a muffled world I do not know.
To open the door was like slicing into a wedding-cake; then,—where was I to put a foot
into that new-laid carpet of ankle-deepness? I
hobbled out in a pair of my uncle's. I suppose it
is because I know every tree and shrub in its
true form that snow seems to pile itself nowhere
as it does here: it becomes a garden of entomb-
ments. Now and then some heap would shuffle
feebly under its shroud, but resurrection was not
to be: the Lawson cypress held out great box-
ing-glove hands for me to shake and set free;
and the silence was wonderful. I padded about
till I froze: this morning I can see my big hoof-
marks all over the place, and Benjy has been
scampering about in them as if he found some
flavor of me there. The trees are already be-

ginning to shake themselves loose, and the spell
is over: but it had a wonderful hold while it
lasted. I take a breath back into last night, and
feel myself again full of a romance without words
that I cannot explain. If you had been there,
even, I think I could have forgotten I had you by
me, the place was so weighed down with its sense
of solitude. It struck eleven while I was outside,
and in that, too, I could hear a muffle as if snow
choked all the belfry lattices and lay even on the
outer edge of the bell itself. Across the park
there are dead boughs cracking down under the
weight of snow; and it would be very like you
to tramp over just because the roads will be so
impossible.

I heard yesterday a thing which made me just
a little more free and easy in mind, though I
had nothing sensibly on my conscience. Such
a good youth who two years ago believed I was
his only possible future happiness, is now quite
happy with a totally different sort of person. I
had a little letter from him, shy and stately, announcing the event. I thought it such a friendly
act, for some have never the grace to unsay their
grievances, however much actually blessed as a
consequence of them.

With that off my mind I can come to you
swearing that there have been no accidents on
anybody's line of life through a mistake in sig-

nals, or a flying in the face of them, where I have had any responsibility. As for you, and as you know well by now, my signals were ready and waiting before you sought for them. "Oh, whistle, and I'll come to you!" was their give-away attitude.

I am going down to play snowballs with Benjy. Good-by. If you come you will find this letter on the hall table, and me you will probably hear barking behind the rhododendrons.—So much your most loving.

## LETTER LIV.

BELOVED: We have been having a great day of tidyings out, rummaging through years and years of accumulations—things quite useless but which I have not liked to throw away. My soul has been getting such dusty answers to all sorts of doubtful inquiries as to where on earth this, that, and the other lay hidden. And there were other things, the memory of which had lain quite dead or slept, till under the light of day they sprouted back into life like corn from the grave of an Egyptian mummy.

Very deep in one box I found a stealthy little collection of secret playthings which it used to be my fond belief that nobody knew of but myself. It may have been Anna's graspingness, when four years of seniority gave her double my age, or Arthur's genial instinct for destructiveness, which drove me into such deep concealment of my dearest idols. But, whether for those or more mystic reasons, I know I had dolls which I nursed only in the strictest privacy and lavished my firmest love upon. It was because of them

that I bore the reproach of being but a lukewarm
mother of dolls and careless of their toilets; the
truth being that my motherly passion expended
itself in secret on certain outcasts of society whom
others despised or had forgotten.   They, on their
limp and dissolute bodies, wore all the finery I
could find to pile on them: and one shady trans-
action done on their behalf I remember now without pangs.   There was one creature of state
whom an inconsiderate relative had presented to
Anna and myself in equal shares.  Of course
Anna's became more and more lionlike.   I had
very little love for the bone. of contention myself, but the sense of injustice rankled in me.
So one day, at an unclothing, Anna discovered
that certain undergarments were gone altogether
away.   She sat aghast, questioned me, and, when
I refused to disgorge, screamed down vengeance
from the authorities.   I was morally certain I
had taken no more than my just share, and resolution sat on my lips under all threats.   For a
punishment the whole ownership of the big doll
was made over to Anna: I was no worse off, and
was very contented with my obstinacy.   To-day
I found the beautifully wrought bodice, which I
had carried beyond reach of even the supreme
court of appeal, clothing with ridiculous loose-
ness a rag-doll whose head tottered on its stem
like an over-ripe plum, and whose legs had no

deportment at all: and am sending it off in charitable surrender to Anna to be given, bag and rag, to whichever one of the children she likes to select.

Also I found:—would you care to have a lock of hair taken from the head of a child then two years old, which, bright golden, does not match what I have on now in the least? I can just remember her: but she is much of a stranger to both of us. Why I value it is that the name and date on the envelope inclosing it are in my mother's handwriting: and I suppose *she* loved very much the curly treasure she then put away. Some of the other things, quite funny, I will show you the next time you come over. How I wish that vanished mite had mixed some of her play-hours with yours:—you only six miles away all the time: had one but known!—Now grown very old and loving, always your own.

## LETTER LV.

BELOVED: I am getting quite out of letter-writing, and it is your doing, not mine. No sooner do I get a line from you than you rush over in person and take the answer to it out of my mouth!

I have had six from you in the last week, and believe I have only exchanged you one: all the rest have been nipped in the bud by your arrivals. My pen turns up a cross nose whenever it hears you coming now, and declares life so dull as not to be worth living. Poor dinky little Othello! it shall have its occupation again to-day, and say just what it likes.

It likes you while you keep away: so that's said! When I make it write "come," it kicks and tries to say "don't." For it is an industrious minion, loves to have work to do, and never complains of overhours. It is a sentimental fact that I keep all its used-up brethren in an inclosure together, and throw none of them away. If once they have ridden over paper to you, I turn them to grass in their old age. I let this out because I think it is time you had another laugh at me.

Laugh, dearest, and tell me that you have done so if you want to make me a little more happy than I have been this last day. or two. There has been too much thinking in the heads of both of us. Be empty-headed for once when you write next: whether you write little or much, I am sure always of your full heart: but I cannot trust your brain to the same pressure: it is such a Martha to headaches and careful about so many things, and you don't bring it here to be soothed as often as you should—not at its most needy moments, I mean.

Have you made the announcement? or does it not go till to-day? I am not sorry, since the move comes from her, that we have not to wait now till February. You will feel better when the storm is up than when it is only looming. This is the headachy period.

Well. Say "well" with me, dearest! It is going to be well: waiting has not suited us—not any of us, I think. Your mother is one in a thousand, I say that and mean it:—worth conquering as all good things are. I would not wish great fortune to come by too primrosy a way. "Canst thou draw out Leviathan with a hook?" Even so, for size, is the share of the world which we lay claim to, and for that we must be toilers of the deep.—Always, Beloved, your truest and most loving.

## LETTER LVI.

My Own Own Love: You have given me a spring day before the buds begin,—the weather I have been longing for! I had been quite sad at heart these cold wet days, really *down;*—a treasonable sadness with you still anywhere in the world (though where in the world have you been?). Spring seemed such a long way off over the bend of it, with you unable to come; and it seems now another letter of yours has got lost. (Write it again, dearest,—all that was in it, with any blots that happened to come:—there was a dear smudge in to-day's, with the whirlpool mark of your thumb quite clear on it,—delicious to rest my face against and feel *you* there.)

And so back to my spring weather: all in a moment you gave me a whole week of the weather I had longed after. For you say the sun has been shining on you: and I would rather have it there than here if it refuses to be in two places at once. Also my letters have pleased you. When they do, I feel such a proud mother to them! Here they fly quick out of the nest; but I think sometimes they must come to you broken-winged, with so much meant and all so badly put.

How can we ever, with our poor handful of senses, contrive to express ourselves perfectly? Perhaps,—I don't know:—dearest, I love you! I kiss you a hundred times to the minute. If everything in the world were dark round us, could not kisses tell us quite well all that we wish to know of each other?—me that you were true and brave and so beautiful that a woman must be afraid looking at you:—and you that I was just my very self,—loving and—no! just loving: I have no room for anything more! You have swallowed up all my moral qualities, I have none left: I am a beggar, where it is so sweet to beg. —Give me back crumbs of myself! I am so hungry, I cannot show it, only by kissing you a hundred times.

Dear share of the world, what a wonderful large helping of it you are to me! I alter Portia's complaint and swear that " my little body is bursting with this great world." And now it is written and I look at it, it seems a Budge and Toddy sort of complaint. I do thank Heaven that the Godhead who rules in it for us does not forbid the recognition of the ludicrous! C—— was telling me how long ago, in her own dull Protestant household, she heard a riddle propounded by some indiscreet soul who did not understand the prudish piety which reigned there: and saw such shocked eyes opening all round on the sound of it. "What is it," was asked, "that a common man can see every day but that God never sees?" "His equal" is the correct answer: but even so demure and proper a support to thistly theology was to the ears that heard it as the hand of Uzzah stretched out intrusively and deserving to be smitten. As for C——, a twinkle of wickedness seized her, she hazarded "A joke" to be the true answer, and was ordered into banishment by the head of that God-fearing household for having so successfully diagnosed the family skeleton.

As for skeletons, why your letter makes me so happy is that the one which has been rubbing its ribs against you for so long seems to have given itself a day off, or crumbled to dissolution. And you are yourself again, as you have not been for many a long day. I suppose there has been thunder, and the air is cleared: and I am not to know any of that side of your discomforts?

Still I *do* know. You have been writing your letters with pressed lips for a month past: and I have been a mere toy-thing, and no helpmate to you at all at all. Oh, why will she not love me? I know I am lovable except to a very hard heart, and hers is not: it is only like yours, reserved in its expression. It is strange what pain her prejudice has been able to drop into my cup of happiness; and into yours, dearest, I fear, even more.

Oh, I love you, I love you! I am crying with it, having no words to declare to you what I feel. My tears have wings in them: first semi-detached, then detached. See, dearest, there is a rain-stain to make this letter fruitful of meaning!

It is sheer convention—and we, creatures of habit—that tears don't come kindly and easily to express where laughter leaves off and a something better begins. Which is all very ungrammatical and entirely me, as I am when I get off my hinges too suddenly.

Amen, amen! When we are both a hundred we shall remember all this very peaceably; and the " sanguine flower " will not look back at us less beautifully because in just one spot it was inscribed with woe. And if we with all our aids cannot have patience, where in this midge-bitten world is that virtue to find a standing?

I kiss you—how? as if it were for the first or the last time? No, but for all time, Beloved! every time I see you or think of you sums up my world. Love me a little, too, and I will be as contented as I am your loving.

## LETTER LVII.

COME to me! I will not understand a word you have written till you come. Who has been using your hand to strike me like this, and why do you lend it? Oh, if it is she, you do not owe her *that* duty! Never write such things:—speak! have you ever found me not listen to you, or hard to convince? Dearest, dearest!—take what I mean: I cannot write over this gulf. Come to me,—I will believe anything you can *say,* but I can believe nothing of this written. I must see you and hear what it is you mean. Dear heart, I am blind till I set eyes on you again! Beloved, I have nothing, nothing in me but love for you: except for that I am empty! Believe me and give me time; I will not be unworthy of the joy of holding you. I am nothing if not *yours!* Tell this to whoever is deceiving you.

Oh, my dearest, why did you stay away from me to write so? Come and put an end to a thing which means nothing to either of us. You love me: how can it have a meaning?

Can you not hear my heart crying?—I love

nobody but you—do not know what love is without you! How can I be more yours than I am?
Tell me, and I will be!

Here are kisses. Do not believe yourself till
you have seen me. Oh, the pain of having to
*write,* of not having your arms round me in my
misery! I kiss your dear blind eyes with all my
heart.—My Love's most loved and loving.

## LETTER LVIII.

No, no, I cannot read it! What have I done that you will not come to me? They are mad here, telling me to be calm, that I am not to go to you. I too am out of my mind—except that I love you. I know nothing except that. Beloved, only on my lips will I take my dismissal from yours: not God himself can claim you from me till you have done me that justice. Kiss me once more, and then, if you can, say we must part. You cannot!—Ah, come here where my heart is, and you cannot!

Have I never told you enough how I love you? Dearest, I have no words for all my love: I have no pride in me. Does not this alone tell you? —You are sending me away, and I cry to you to spare me. Can I love you more than that? What will you have of me that I have not given? Oh, you, the sun in my dear heavens —if I lose you, what is left of me? Could you break so to pieces even a woman you did not love? And me you *do* love,—you *do*. Between all this denial of me, and all this silence of words that you have put your name to, I see clearly that you are still my lover. —Your writing breaks with trying not to say it: you say again and again that there is no fault in me. I swear to you, dearest, there is none, unless it be loving you: and how can you mean that? For what are you and I made for unless for each other? With all our difference people tell us we are alike. We were shaped for each other from our very birth. Have we not proved it in a hundred days of happiness, which have lifted us up to the blue of a heaven higher than any birds ever sang? And now you say—taking on you the blame for the very life-blood in us both—that the fault is yours, and that your fault is to have allowed me to love you and yourself to love me!

Who has suddenly turned our love into a crime? Beloved, is it a sin that here on earth I have been seeing God through you? Go away from me, and He is gone also. Ah, sweetheart, let me see you before all my world turns into a wilderness! Let me know better why,—if my senses are to be emptied of you. My heart can never let you go. Do you wish that it should?

Bring your own here, and see if it can tell me that! Come and listen to mine! Oh, dearest heart that ever beat, mine beats so like yours that once together you shall not divide their sound!

Beloved, I will be patient, believe me, to any words you can say: but I cannot be patient away from you. If I have seemed to reproach you, do not think that now. For you are to give me a greater joy than I ever had before when you take me in your arms again after a week that has spelled dreadful separation. And I shall bless you for it—for this present pain even—because the joy will be so much greater.

Only come: I do not live till you have kissed me again. Oh, my beloved, how cruel love may seem if we do not trust it enough! My trust in you has come back in a great rush of warmth, like a spring day after frost. I almost laugh as I let this go. It brings you,—perhaps before I wake: I shall be so tired to-night. Call under my window, make me hear in my sleep. I will wake up to you, and it shall be all over before the rest of the world wakes. There is no dream so deep that I shall not hear you out of the midst of it. Come and be my morning-glory to-morrow without fail. I will rewrite nothing that I have written—let it go! See me out of deep waters again, because I have thought so much of you! I have come through clouds and thick darkness. I press your name to my lips a thousand times. As sure as sunrise I say to myself that you will come: the sun is not truer to his rising than you to me.

Love will go flying after this till I sleep.   God bless you!—and me also; it is all one and the same wish.—Your most true, loving, and dear faithful one.

## LETTER LIX.

I HAVE to own that I know your will now, at last. Without seeing you I am convinced: you have a strong power in you to have done that! You have told me the word I am to say to you: it is your bidding, so I say it—Good-by. But it is a word whose meaning I cannot share.

Yet I have something to tell you which I could not have dreamed if it had not somehow been true: which has made it possible for me to believe, without hearing you speak it, that I am to be dismissed out of your heart.—May the doing of it cost you far less pain than I am fearing!

You did not come, though I promised myself so certainly that you would: instead came your last very brief note which this is to obey. Still I watched for you to come, believing it still and trusting to silence on my part to bring you more certainly than any more words could do. And at last either you came to me, or I came to you: a bitter last meeting. Perhaps your mind too holds what happened, if so I have got truly at what your will is. I must accept it as true, since I am not to see you again. I cannot tell you whether I thought it or dreamed it, but it seems still quite real, and has turned all my past life into a mockery.

When I came I was behind you; then you turned and I could see your face—you too were in pain: in that we seemed one. But when I touched you and would have kissed you, you shuddered at me and drew back your head. I tell you this as I would tell you anything unbelievable that I had heard told of you behind your back. You see I am obeying you at last.

For all the love which you gave me when I seemed worthy of it I thank you a thousand times. Could you ever return to the same mind, I should be yours once more as I still am; never ceasing on my side to be your lover and servant till death, and—if there be anything more—after as well.

My lips say amen now: but my heart cannot say it till breath goes out of my body. Good-by: that means—God be with you. I mean it; but He seems to have ceased to be with me altogether. Good-by, dearest. I kiss your heart with writing for the last time, and your eyes, that

will see nothing more from me after this.
Good-by.

NOTE.—All the letters which follow were found lying loosely together. They only went to their destination after the writer's death.

## LETTER LX.

To-day, dearest, a letter from you reached me: a fallen star which had lost its way. It lies dead in my bosom. It was the letter that lost itself in the post while I was traveling: it comes now with half a dozen postmarks, and signs of long waiting in one place. In it you say, " We have been engaged now for two whole months; I never dreamed that two moons could contain so much happiness." Nor I, dearest! We have now been separated for three; and till now I had not dreamed that time could so creep, to such infinitely small purpose, as it has in carrying me from the moment when I last saw you.

You were so dear to me, Beloved; *that* you ever are! Time changes nothing in you as you seemed to me then. Oh, I am sick to touch your hands: all my thoughts run to your service: they seem to hear you call, only to find locked doors.

If you could see me now I think you would open the door for a little while.

If they came and told me—" You are to see him just for five minutes, and then part again " —what should I be wanting most to say to you?

Nothing—only " Speak, speak! " I would have you fill my heart with your voice the whole time: five minutes more of you to fold my life round. It would matter very little what you said, barring the one thing that remains never to be said.

Oh, could all this silence teach me the one thing I am longing to know!—why am I unworthy of you? If I cannot be your wife, why cannot I see you still,—serve you if possible? I would be grateful.

You meant to be generous; and wishing not to wound me, you said that " there was no fault " in me. I realize now that you would not have said that to the woman you still loved. And now I am never to know what part in me is hateful to you. I must live with it because you would not tell me the truth!

Every day tells me I am different from the thing I wish to be—your love, the woman you approve.

I love you, I love you! Can I get no nearer to you ever for all this straining? If I love you so much, I must be moving toward what you would have me be. In our happiest days my heart had its growing pains,—growing to be as you wished it.

Dear, even the wisest make mistakes, and the tenderest may be hard without knowing: I do not think I am unworthy of you, if you knew all.

Writing to you now seems weakness: yet it seemed peace to come in here and cry to you. And when I go about I have still strength left, and try to be cheerful. Nobody knows, I think nobody knows. No one in the house is made downcast because of me. How dear they are, and how little I can thank them! Except to you, dearest, I have not shown myself selfish.

I love you too much, too much: I cannot write it.

## LETTER LXI.

You are very ill, they tell me. Beloved, it is such kindness in them to have regard for the wish they disapprove and to let me know. Knowledge is the one thing needful whose lack has deprived me of my happiness: the express image of sorrow is not so terrible as the foreboding doubt of it. Not because you are ill, but because I know something definitely about you, I am happier to-day: a little nearer to a semblance of service to you in my helplessness. How much I wish you well, even though that might again carry you out of my knowledge! And, though death might bring you nearer than life now makes possible, I pray to you, dearest, not to die. It is not right that you should die yet, with a mistake in your heart which a little more life might clear away.

Praying for your dear eyes to remain open, I realize suddenly how much hope still remains in me, where I thought none was left. Even your illness I take as a good omen; and the thought of you weak as a child and somewhat like one in your present state with no brain for deep thinking, comes to my heart to be cherished endlessly: there you lie, Beloved, brought home to my imagination as never since the day we parted. And the thought comes to the rescue of my helpless longing—that it is as little children that men get brought into the kingdom of Heaven. Let that be the medicine and outcome of your sickness, my own Beloved! I hold my breath with hope that I shall have word of you when your hand has strength again to write. For I know that in sleepless nights and in pain you will be unable not to think of me. If you made resolutions against that when you were well, they will go now that you are laid weak; and so some power will come back to me, and my heart will never be asleep for thinking that yours lies awake wanting it:—nor ever be at rest for devising ways by which to be at the service of your conscious longing.

Ah, my own one Beloved, whom I have loved so openly and so secretly, if you were as I think some other men are, I could believe that I had given you so much of my love that you had tired of me because I had made no favor of it but had let you see that I was your faithful subject and servant till death: so that after twenty years you, chancing upon an empty day in your life, might come back and find me still yours;—as to-morrow, if you came, you would.

My pride died when I saw love looking out of
your eyes at me; and it has not come back to me
now that I see you no more. I have no wish that
it should. In all ways possible I would wish to
be as I was when you loved me; and seek to
change nothing except as you bid me.

## LETTER LXII.

So I have seen you, Beloved, again, after fearing that I never should.  A day's absence from home has given me this great fortune.

The pain of it was less than it might have been, since our looks did not meet.  To have seen your eyes shut out their recognition of me would have hurt me too much: I must have cried out against such a judgment.  But you passed by the window without knowing, your face not raised: so little changed, yet you have been ill.  Arthur tells me everything: he knows I must have any word of you that goes begging.

Oh, I hope you are altogether better, happier! An illness helps some people: the worst of their sorrow goes with the health that breaks down under it; and they come out purged into a clearer air, and are made whole for a fresh trial of life.

I hear that you are going quite away; and my eyes bless this chance to have embraced you once again.  Your face is the kindest I have ever seen:

even your silence, while I looked at you, seemed a grace instead of a cruelty. What kindness, I say to myself, even if it be mistaken kindness, must have sealed those dear lips not to tell me of my unworth!

Oh, if I could see once into the brain of it all! No one but myself knows how good you are: how can I, then, be so unworthy of you? Did you think I would not surrender to anything you fixed, that you severed us so completely, not even allowing us to meet, and giving me no way to come back to you though I might come to be all that you wished? Ah, dear face, how hungry you have made me!—the more that I think you are not yet so happy as I could wish,—as I could make you,—I say it foolishly:—yet if you would trust me, I am sure.

Oh, how tired loving you now makes me! physically I grow weary with the ache to have you in my arms. And I dream, I dream always, the shadows of former kindness that never grow warm enough to clasp me before I wake.—Yours, dearest, waking or sleeping.

## LETTER LXIII.

Do you remember, Beloved, when you came on your birthday, you said I was to give you another birthday present of your own choosing, and I promised? And it was that we were to do for the whole day what *I* wished: you were not to be asked to choose.

You said then that it was the first time I had ever let you have your way, which was to see me be myself independently of you:—as if such a self existed.

You will never see what I write now; and I did not do then any of the things I most wished: for first I wished to kneel down and kiss your hands and feet; and you would not have liked that. Even now that you love me no more, you would not like me to do such a thing. A woman can never do as she likes when she loves—there is no such thing until he shows it her or she divines it. I loved you, I loved you!—that was all I could do, and all I wanted to do.

You have kept my letters? Do you read them ever, I wonder? and do they tell you differently about me, now that you see me with new eyes? Ah no, you dare not look at them: they tell too much truth! How can love-letters ever cease to be the winged things they were when they first came? I fancy mine sick to death for want of your heart to rest on; but never less loving.

If you would read them again, you would come back to me. Those little throats of happiness would be too strong for you. And so you lay them in a cruel grave of lavender,—" Lavender for forgetfulness " might be another song for Ophelia to sing.

I am weak with writing to you, I have written too long: this is twice to-day.

I do not write to make myself more miserable: only to fill up my time.

When I go about something definite, I can do it:—to ride, or read aloud to the old people, or sit down at meals with them is very easy; but I cannot make employment for myself—that requires too much effort of invention and will: and I have only will for one thing in life—to get through it: and no invention to the purpose. Oh, Beloved, in the grave I shall lie forever with a lock of your hair in my hand. I wonder if, beyond there, one sees anything? My eyes ache to-day from the brain, which is always at blind groping for you, and the point where I missed you.

## LETTER LXIV.

DEAREST: It is dreadful to own that I was glad at first to know that you and your mother were no longer together, glad of something that must mean pain to you! I am not now. When you were ill I did a wrong thing: from her something came to me which I returned. I would do much to undo that act now; but this has fixed it forever. With it were a few kind words. I could not bear to accept praise from her: all went back to her! Oh, poor thing, poor thing! if I ever had an enemy I thought it was she! I do not think so now. Those who seem cold seldom are. I hope you were with her at the last: she loved you beyond any word that was in her nature to utter, and the young are hard on the old without knowing it. We were two people, she and I, whose love clashed jealously over the same object, and we both failed. She is the first to get rest.

## LETTER LXV.

MY DEAR: I dream of you now every night, and you are always kind, always just as I knew you: the same without a shadow of change.

I cannot picture you anyhow else, though my life is full of the silence you have made. My heart seems to have stopped on the last beat the sight of your handwriting gave it.

I dare not bid you come back now: sorrow has made me a stranger to myself. I could not look at you and say " I am your Star ":—I could not believe it if I said it. Two women have inhabited me, and the one here now is not the one you knew and loved: their one likeness is that they both have loved the same man, the one certain that her love was returned, and the other certain of nothing. What a world of difference lies in that!

I lay hands on myself, half doubting, and feel my skeleton pushing to the front: my glass shows it me. Thus we are all built up: bones are at the foundations of our happiness, and when the happiness wears thin, they show through, the true architecture of humanity.

I have to realize now that I have become the greatest possible failure in life,—a woman who has lost her " share of the world ": I try to shape myself to it.

It is deadly when a woman's sex, what was once her glory, reveals itself to her as an all-containing loss. I realized myself fully only when I was with you; and now I can't undo it.— You gone, I lean against a shadow, and feel myself forever falling, drifting to no end, a Francesca without a Paolo. Well, it must be some comfort that I do not drag you with me. I never believed myself a " strong " woman; your lightest wish shaped me to its liking. Now you have molded me with your own image and superscription, and have cast me away.

Are not the die and the coin that comes from it only two sides of the same form?—there is not a hair's breadth anywhere between their surfaces where they lie, the one inclosing the other. Yet part them, and the light strikes on them how differently! That is a mere condition of light: join them in darkness, where the light cannot strike, and they are the same—two faces of a single form. So you and I, dear, when we are dead, shall come together again, I trust. Or are we to come back to each other defaced and warped out of our true conjunction? I think not: for if you have changed, if soul can ever change, I shall be melted again by your touch, and flow to meet all the change that is in you, since my true self is to be you.

Oh, you, my Beloved, do you wake happy, either with or without thoughts of me? I cannot understand, but I trust that it may be so. If I could have a reason why I have so passed out of your life, I could endure it better. What was in me that you did not wish? What was in you that I must not wish for evermore? If the root of this separation was in you, if in God's will it was ordered that we were to love, and, without loving less, afterwards be parted, I could acquiesce so willingly. But it is this knowing nothing that overwhelms me:—I strain my eyes for sight and can't see; I reach out my hands for the sunlight and am given great handfuls of darkness. I said to you the sun had dropped out of my heaven.—My dear, my dear, is this darkness indeed you? Am I in the mold with my face to yours, receiving the close impression of a misery in which we are at one? Are you, dearest, hungering and thirsting for me, as I now for you?

I wonder what, to the starving and drought-stricken, the taste of death can be like! Do all the rivers of the world run together to the lips then, and all its fruits strike suddenly to the taste

when the long deprivation ceases to be a want?
Or is it simply a ceasing of hunger and thirst—
an antidote to it all?

I may know soon. How very strange if at the
last I forget to think of you!

## LETTER LXVI.

DEAREST : Every day I am giving myself a little more pain than I need—for the sake of you. I am giving myself your letters to read again day by day as I received them. Only one a day, so that I have still something left to look forward to to-morrow : and oh, dearest, what *unanswerable* things they have now become, those letters which I used to answer so easily! There is hardly a word but the light of to-day stands before it like a drawn sword, between the heart that then felt and wrote so, and mine as it now feels and waits.

All your tenderness then seems to be cruelty now : only *seems,* dearest, for I still say, I *do* say that it is not so. I know it is not so : I, who know nothing else, know that! So I look every day at one of these monstrous contradictions, and press it to my heart till it becomes reconciled with the pain that is there always.

Indeed you loved me : that I see now. Words which I took so much for granted then have a strange force now that I look back at them. You did love : and I who did not realize it enough then, realize it now when you no longer do,

And the commentary on all this is that one letter of yours which I say over and over to myself sometimes when I cannot pray: "There is no fault in you: the fault is elsewhere; I can no longer love you as I did. All that was between us must be at an end; for your good and mine the only right thing is to say good-by without meeting. I know you will not forget me, but you will forgive me, even because of the great pain I cause you. You are the most generous woman I have known. If it would comfort you to blame me for this I would beg you to do it: but I know you better, and ask you to believe that it is my deep misfortune rather than my fault that I can be no longer your lover, as, God knows, I was once, I dare not say how short a time ago. To me you remain, what I always found you, the best and most true-hearted woman a man could pray to meet."

This, dearest, I say and say: and write down now lest you have forgotten it. For your writing of it, and all the rest of you that I have, goes with me to my grave. How superstitious we are of our own bodies after death!—I, as if I believed that I should ever rise or open my ears to any sound again! I do not, yet it comforts me to make sure that certain things shall go with me to dissolution.

Truly, dearest, I believe grief is a great deceiver, and that no one quite quite wishes not to exist. I have no belief in future existence; yet I wish it so much—to exist again outside all this failure of my life. For at present I have done you no good at all, only evil.

And I hope now and then, that writing thus to you I am not writing altogether in vain. If I can see sufficiently at the last to say—Send him these, it will be almost like living again: for surely you will love me again when you see how much I have suffered,—and suffered because I would not let thought of you go.

Could you dream, Beloved, reading *this* that there is bright sunlight streaming over my paper as I write?

## LETTER LXVII.

Do you forgive me for coming into your life, Beloved? I do not know in what way I can have hurt you, but I know that I have. Perhaps without knowing it we exchange salves for the wounds we have given and received? Dearest, I trust those I send reach you: I send them, wishing till I grow weak. My arms strain and become tired trying to be wings to carry them to you: and I am glad of that weariness—it seems to be some virtue that has gone out of me. If all my body could go out in the effort, I think I should get a glimpse of your face, and the meaning of everything then at last.

I have brought in a wild rose to lay here in love's cenotaph, among all my thoughts of you. It comes from a graveyard full of " little deaths." I remember once sending you a flower from the same place when love was still fortunate with us. I must have been reckless in my happiness to do that!

Beloved, if I could speak or write out all my thoughts, till I had emptied myself of them, I feel that I should rest.   But there is no *emptying* the brain by thinking.   Things thought come to be thought again over and over, and more and fresh come in their train: children and grand-children, generations of them, sprung from the old stock.   I have many thoughts now, born of my love for you, that never came when we were together,—grandchildren of our days of court-ship.   Some of them are set down here, but others escape and will never see your face!

If (poor word, it has the sound but no hope of a future life): still, IF you should ever come back to me and want, as you would want, to know something of the life in between,—I could put these letters that I keep into your hands and trust them to say for me that no day have I been truly, that is to say *willingly*, out of your heart. When Richard Feverel comes back to his wife, do you remember how she takes him to see their child, which till then he had never seen—and its likeness to him as it lies asleep?   Dearest, have I not been as true to you in all that I leave here written?

If, when I come to my finish, I get any truer glimpse of your mind, and am sure of what you would wish, I will leave word that these shall be sent to you.   If not, I must suppose knowledge is still delayed, not that it will not reach you.

Sometimes I try still not to wish to die.   For

my poor body's sake I wish Well to have its last chance of coming to pass. It is the unhappy unfulfilled clay of life, I think, which robbed of its share of things set ghosts to walk: mists which rise out of a ground that has not worked out its fruitfulness, to take the shape of old desires. If I leave a ghost, it will take *your* shape, not mine, dearest: for it will be "as trees walking" that the "lovers of trees" will come back to earth. Browning did not know that. Someone else, not Browning, has worded it for us: a lover of trees far away sends his soul back to the country that has lost him, and there "the traveler, marveling why, halts on the bridge to hearken how soft the poplars sigh," not knowing that it is the lover himself who sighs in the trees all night. That is how the ghosts of real love come back into the world. The ghosts of love and the ghosts of hatred must be quite different: these bring fear, and those none. Come to me, dearest, in the blackest night, and I will not be afraid.

How strange that when one has suffered most, it is the poets (those who are supposed to *sing*) who best express things for us. Yet singing is the thing I feel least like. If ever a heart once woke up to find itself full of tune, it was mine; now you have drawn all the song out of it, emptied it dry: and I go to the poets to read epitaphs.

I think it is their cruelty that appeals to me:—
they can sing of grief! O hard hearts!

Sitting here thinking of you, my ears have
suddenly become wide open to the night-sounds
outside. A night-jar is making its beautiful burr
in the stillness, and there are things going away
and away, telling me the whereabouts of life like
points on a map made for the ear. You, too, are
*somewhere* outside, making no sound: and listen-
ing for you I heard these. It seemed as if my
brain had all at once opened and caught a new
sense. Are you there? This is one of those
things which drop to us with no present meaning: yet I know I am not to forget it as long as
I live.

Good-night! At your head, at your feet, is
there any room for me to-night, Beloved?

## LETTER LXVIII.

DEAREST: The thought keeps troubling me how to give myself to you most, if you should ever come back for me when I am no longer here. These poor letters are all that I can leave: will they tell you enough of my heart?

Oh, into that, wish any wish that you like, and it is there already! My heart, dearest, only moves in the wish to be what you desire.

Yet I am conscious that I cannot give, unless you shall choose to take: and though I write myself down each day your willing slave, I cry my wares in a market where there is no bidder to hear me.

Dearest, though my whole life is yours, it is little you know of it. My wish would be to have every year of my life blessed by your consciousness of it. Barely a year of me is all that you have, truly, to remember: though I think five summers at least came to flower, and withered in that one.

I wish you knew my whole life: I cannot tell it: it was too full of infinitely small things. Yet what I can remember I would like to tell now: so that some day, perhaps, perhaps, my childhood may here and there be warmed long after its death by your knowledge coming to it and discovering in it more than you knew before.

How I long, dearest, that what I write may look up some day and meet your eye! Beloved, *then*, however faded the ink may have grown, I think the spirit of my love will remain fresh in it:—I kiss you on the lips with every word. The thought of " good-by " is never to enter here: it is *A reviderci* for ever and ever:— " Love, love," and " meet again! "—the words we put into the thrush's song on a day you will remember, when all the world for us was a garden.

Dearest, what I can tell you of older days,— little things they must be—I will: and I know that if you ever come to value them at all, their littleness will make them doubly welcome:—just as to know that you were once called a " gallous young hound " by people whom you plagued when a boy, was to me a darling discovery: all at once I caught my childhood's imaginary comrade to my young spirit's heart and kissed him, brow and eyes.

Good-night, good-night! To-morrow I will find you some earliest memory: the dew of Hermon be on it when you come to it—if ever!

Oh, Beloved, could you see into my heart now, or I into yours, time would grow to nothing for us; and my childhood would stay unwritten!

From far and near I gather my thoughts of you for the kiss I cannot give. Good-night, dearest.

## LETTER LXIX.

BELOVED: I remember my second birthday. I am quite sure of it, because my third I remember so infinitely well.—Then I was taken in to see Arthur lying in baby bridal array of lace fringes and gauze, and received in my arms held up for me by Nan-nan the awful weight and imperial importance of his small body.

I think from the first I was told of him as my "brother": cousin I have never been able to think him. But all this belongs to my third: on my second, I remember being on a floor of roses; and they told me if I would go across to a cupboard and pull it open there would be something there waiting for me. And it was on all-fours that I went all eagerness across great patches of rose-pattern, till I had butted my way through a door left ajar, and found in a cardboard box of bright tinsel and flowers two little wax babes in the wood lying.

I think they gave me my first sense of color, except, perhaps, the rose-carpet which came earlier, and they remained for quite a long time the most beautiful thing I knew. It is strange that I cannot remember what became of them, for I am sure I neither broke nor lost them,—perhaps it was done for me: Arthur came afterward, the tomb of many of my early joys, and the maker of so many new ones. He, dearest, is the one, the only one, who has seen the tears that belong truly to you: and he blesses me with such wonderful patience when I speak your name, allowing that perhaps I know better than he. And after the wax babies I had him for my third birthday.

## LETTER LXX.

BELOVED: I think that small children see very much as animals must do: just the parts of things which have a direct influence on their lives, and no memory outside that. I remember the kindness or frowns of faces in early days far more than the faces themselves: and it is quite a distinct and later memory that I have of standing within a doorway and watching my mother pass downstairs unconscious of my being there,—and *then*, for the first time, studying her features and seeing in them a certain solitude and distance which I had never before noticed:—I suppose because I had never before thought of looking at her when she was not concerned with me.

It was this unobservance of actual features, I imagine, which made me think all gray-haired people alike, and find a difficulty in recognizing those who called, except generically as callers— people who kissed me, and whom therefore I liked to see.

One, I remember, for no reason unless because she had a brown face, I mistook from a distance

for my Aunt Dolly, and bounded into the room
where she was sitting, with a cry of rapture.
And it was my earliest conscious test of politeness, when I found out my mistake, not to cry
over it in the kind but very inferior presence to
that one I had hoped for.

I suppose, also, that many sights which have
no meaning to children go, happily, quite out of
memory; and that what our early years leave for
us in the mind's lavender are just the tit-bits of
life, or the first blows to our intelligence—things
which did matter and mean much.

Corduroys come early into my life,—their
color and the queer earthy smell of those which
particularly concerned me: because I was picked
up from a fall and tenderly handled by a rough
working-man so clothed, whom I regarded for
a long time afterward as an adorable object. He
and I lived to my recognition of him as a wiz-
ened, scrubby, middle-aged man, but remained
good friends after the romance was over. I
don't know when the change in my sense of
beauty took place as regards him.

Anything unusual that appealed to my senses
left exaggerated marks. My father once in full
uniform appeared to me as a giant, so that I
screamed and ran, and required much of his kindest voice to coax me back to him.

Also once in the street a dancer in fancy costume struck me in the same way, and seemed in his red tunic twice the size of the people who crowded round him.

I think as a child the small ground-flowers of spring took a larger hold upon me than any others:—I was so close to them. Roses I don't remember till I was four or five; but crocus and snowdrop seem to have been in my blood from the very beginning of things; and I remember likening the green inner petals of the snowdrop to the skirts of some ballet-dancing dolls, which danced themselves out of sight before I was four years old.

Snapdragons, too, I remember as if with my first summer: I used to feed them with bits of their own green leaves, believing faithfully that those mouths must need food of some sort. When I became more thoughtful I ceased to make cannibals of them: but I think I was less convinced then of the digestive process. I don't know when I left off feeding snapdragons: I think calceolarias helped to break me off the habit, for I found they had no throats to swallow with.

In much the same way as sights that have no meaning leave no traces, so I suppose do words and sounds. It was many years before I over-heard, in the sense of taking in, a conversation by elders not meant for me: though once, in my innocence, I hid under the table during the elders' late dinner, and came out at dessert, to which we were always allowed to come down, hoping to be an amusing surprise to them. And I could not at all understand why I was scolded; for, indeed, I had *heard* nothing at all, though no doubt plenty that was unsuitable for a child's ears had been said, and was on the elder's minds when they upbraided me.

Dearest, such a long-ago! and all these smallest of small things I remember again, to lay them up for you: all the child-parentage of me whom you loved once, and will again if ever these come to you.

Bless my childhood, dearest: it did not know it was lonely of you, as I know of myself now! And yet I have known you, and know you still, so am the more blest.—Good-night.

## LETTER LXXI.

I USED to stand at the foot of the stairs a long time, when by myself, before daring to start up: and then it was always the right foot that went first. And a fearful feeling used to accompany me that I was going to meet the " evil chance " when I got to the corner. Sometimes when I felt it was there very badly, I used at the last moment to shut my eyes and walk through it: and feel, on the other side, like a pilgrim who had come through the waters of Jordan.

My eyes were always the timidest things about me: and to shut my eyes tight against the dark was the only way I had of meeting the solitude of the first hour of bed when Nan-nan had left me, and before I could get to sleep.

I have an idea that one listens better with one's eyes shut, and that this and other things are a remnant of our primitive existence when perhaps the ears of our arboreal ancestors kept a lookout while the rest of their senses slept. I think, also, that the instinct I found in myself, and have since in other children, to conceal a wound is a similar survival. At one time, I suppose, in the human herd the damaged were quickly put out of existence; and it was the self-preservation instinct which gave me so keen a wish to get into hiding when one day I cut my finger badly—something more than a mere scratch, which I would have cried over and had bandaged quite in the correct way. I remember I sat in a corner and pretended to be nursing a rag doll which I had knotted round my hand, till Nan-nan noticed, perhaps, that I looked white, and found blood flowing into my lap. And I can recall still the overcoming comfort which fell upon me as I let resolution go, and sobbed in her arms full of pity for myself and scolding the "naughty knife" that had done the deed. The rest of that day is lost to me.

Yet it is not only occasions of happiness and pain which impress themselves. When the mind takes a sudden stride in consciousness,—that, also, fixes itself. I remember the agony of shyness which came on me when strange hands did my undressing for me once in Nan-nan's absence: the first time I had felt such a thing. And another day I remember, after contemplating the head of Judas in a pictorial puzzle for a long time, that I seized a brick and pounded him with it beyond recognition:—these were the first vengeful beginnings of Christianity in me. All my history, Bible and English, came to me through picture-books. I wept tenderly over the endangered eyes of Prince Arthur, yet I put out the eyes of many kings, princes, and governors who incurred my displeasure, scratching them with pins till only a white blur remained on the paper.

All this comes to me quite seriously now: I used to laugh thinking it over. But can a single thing we do be called trivial, since out of it we grow up minute by minute into a whole being charged with capacity for gladness or suffering?

Now, as I look back, all these atoms of memory are dust and ashes that I have walked through in order to get to present things. How I suffer, how I suffer! If you could have dreamed that a human body could contain so much suffering, I think you would have chosen a less dreadful way of showing me your will: you would have given me a reason why I have to suffer so.

Dearest, I am broken off every habit I ever had, except my love of you. If you would come back to me you could shape me into whatever you wished. I will be different in all but just that one thing.

## LETTER LXXII.

HERE in my pain, Beloved, I remember keenly now the one or two occasions when as a small child I was consciously a cause of pain to others. What an irony of life that once of the two times when I remember to have been cruel, it was to Arthur, with his small astonished baby-face remaining a reproach to me ever after! I was hardly five then, and going up to the nursery from downstairs had my supper-cake in my hand, only a few mouthfuls left. He had been having his bath, and was sitting up on Nan-nan's knee being got into his bed clothes; when spying me with my cake he piped to have a share of it. I dare say it would not have been good for him, but of that I thought nothing at all: the cruel impulse took me to make one mouthful of all that was left. He watched it go without crying; but his eyes opened at me in a strange way, wondering at this sudden lesson of the hardness of a human heart. "All gone!" was what he said, turning his head from me up to Nan-nan, to see perhaps if she too had a like surprise for

his wee intelligence. I think I have never for-
given myself that, though Arthur has no memory of it left in him: the judging remembrance of
it would, I believe, win forgiveness to him for
any wrong he might now do me, if that and not
the contrary were his way with me: so unrea-
sonably is my brain scarred where the thought of
it still lies. God may forgive us our trespasses
by marvelous slow ways; but we cannot always
forgive them ourselves.

The other thing came out of a less personal
greed, and was years later: Arthur and I were
collecting eggs, and in the loft over one of the
out-houses there was a swallow's nest too high
up to be reached by any ladder we could get up
there. I was intent on getting the *eggs*, and
thought of no other thing that might chance: so
I spread a soft fall below, and with a long pole
I broke the floor of the nest. Then with a sudden stir of horror I saw soft things falling along
with the clay, tiny and feathery. Two were
killed by the breakage that fell with them, but
one was quite alive and unhurt. I gathered up
the remnants of the nest and set it with the
young one in it by the loft window where the
parent-birds might see, making clumsy strivings
of pity to quiet my conscience. The parent-
birds did see, soon enough: they returned, first
up to the rafters, then darting round and round

and crying; then to where their little one lay
helpless and exposed, hung over it with a nib-
bling movement of their beaks for a moment,
making my miserable heart bound up with hope:
then away, away, shrieking into the July sunshine. Once they came back, and shrieked at
the horror of it all, and fled away not to return.

I remained for hours and did whatever silly
pity could dictate: but of course the young one
died: and I—*cleared away all remains that nobody might see!* And that I gave up egg-col-
lecting after that was no penance, but choice.
Since then the poignancy of my regret when I
think of it has never softened. The question
which pride of life and love of make-believe till
then had not raised in me, "Am I a god to kill
and to make alive?" was answered all at once
by an emphatic "No," which I never afterward
forgot. But the grief remained all the same, that
life, to teach me that blunt truth, should have
had to make sacrifice in the mote-hung loft of
three frail lives on a clay-altar, and bring to nothing but pain and a last miserable dart away into
the bright sunshine the spring work of two swift-
winged intelligences. Is man, we are told to
think, not worth many sparrows? Oh, Beloved,
sometimes I doubt it! and would in thought give
my life that those swallows in their generations
might live again.

Beloved, I am letting what I have tried to tell you of my childhood end in a sad way. For it is no use, no use: I have not to-day a glimmer of hope left that your eyes will ever rest on what I have been at such deep trouble to write.

If I were being punished for these two childish things I did, I should see a side of justice in it all. But it is for loving you I am being punished: and not God himself shall make me let you go! Beloved, Beloved, all my days are at your feet, and among them days when you held me to your heart. Good-night; good-night always now!

## LETTER LXXIII.

DEAREST: I could never have made any appeal *from* you to anybody: all my appeal has been *to* you alone. I have wished to hear reason from no other lips but yours; and had you but really and deeply confided in me, I believe I could have submitted almost with a light heart to what you thought best:—though in no way and by no stretch of the imagination can I see you coming to me for the last time and *saying*, as you only wrote, that it was best we should never see each other again.

You could not have said that with any sound of truth; and how can it look truer frozen into writing? I have kissed the words, because you wrote them; not believing them. It is a suspense of unbelief that you have left me in, oh, still dearest! Yet never was sad heart truer to the fountain of all its joy than mine to yours. You had only to see me to know that.

Some day, I dream, we shall come suddenly together, and you will see, before a word, before I have time to gather my mind back to the bodily comfort of your presence, a face filled with thoughts of you that have never left it, and never been bitter:—I believe never once bitter. For even when I think, and convince myself that you have wronged yourself—and so, me also,—even then: oh, then most of all, my heart seems to break with tenderness, and my spirit grow more famished than ever for the want of you! For if you have done right, wisely, then you have no longer any need of me: but if you have done wrong, then you must need me. Oh, dear heart, let that need overwhelm you like a sea, and bring you toward me on its strong tide! And come when you will I shall be waiting.

## LETTER LXXIV.

DEAREST AND DEAREST: So long as you are still this to my heart I trust to have strength to write it; though it is but a ghost of old happiness that comes to me in the act. I have no hope now left in me: but I love you not less, only more, if that be possible: or is it the same love with just a weaker body to contain it all? I find that to have definitely laid off all hope gives me a certain relief: for now that I am so hopeless it becomes less hard not to misjudge you— not to say and think impatiently about you things which would explain why I had to die like this.

Dearest, nothing but love shall explain anything of you to me. When I think of your dear face, it is only love that can give it its meaning. If love would teach me the meaning of this silence, I would accept all the rest, and not ask for any joy in life besides. For if I had the meaning, however dark, it would be by love speaking to me again at last; and I should have your hand holding mine in the darkness forever.

Your face, Beloved, I can remember so well that it would be enough if I had your hand:— the meaning, just the meaning, why I have to sit blind.

## LETTER LXXV.

DEAREST: There is always one possibility
which I try to remember in all I write: even
where there is no hope a thing remains *possible:*
—that your eye may some day come to rest upon
what I leave here. And I would have nothing
so dark as to make it seem that I were better
dead than to have come to such a pass through
loving you. If I felt that, dearest, I should not
be writing my heart out to you, as I do: when
I cease doing that I shall indeed have become
dead and not want you any more, I suppose.
How far I am from dying, then, now!

So be quite sure that if now, even now,—for
to-day of all days has seemed most dark—if now
I were given my choice—to have known you or
not to have known you,—Beloved, a thousand
times I would claim to keep what I have, rather
than have it taken away from me. I cannot forget that for a few months I was the happiest
woman I ever knew: and that happiness is perhaps only by present conditions removed from
me. If I have a soul, I believe good will come

back to it; because I have done nothing to deserve this darkness unless by loving you: and if *by* loving you, I am glad that the darkness came.

Beloved, you have the yes and no to all this: *I* have not, and cannot have. Something that you have not chosen for me to know, you know: it should be a burden on your conscience, surely, not to have shared it with me. Maybe there is something I know that you do not. In the way of sorrow, I think and wish—yes. In the way of love, I wish to think—no.

Any more thinking wearies me. Perhaps we have loved too much, and have lost our way out of our poor five senses, without having strength to take over the new world which is waiting beyond them. Well, I would rather, Beloved, suffer through loving too much, than through loving too little. It is a good fault as faults go. And it is *my* fault, Beloved: so some day you may have to be tender to it.

## LETTER LXXVJ.

DEAREST: I feel constantly that we are together still: I cannot explain. When I am most
miserable, even so that I feel a longing to fly out
of reach of the dear household voices which say
shy things to keep me cheerful,—I feel that I
have you in here waiting for me. Heart's heart,
in my darkest, it is you who speak to me!

As I write I have my cheek pressed against
yours. None of it is true: not a word, not a day
that has separated us! I am yours: it is only the
poor five senses part of us that spells absence.
Some day, some day you will answer this letter
which has to stay locked in my desk. Some
day, I mean, an answer will reach me:—without
your reading this, your answer will come. Is
not your heart at this moment answering me?

Dearest, I trust you: I could not have dreamed
you to myself, therefore you must be true, quite
independently of me. You as I saw you once
with open eyes remain so forever. You cannot
make yourself, Beloved, not to be what you are:
you have called my soul to life if for no other

reason than to bear witness of you, come what may. No length of silence can make a truth once sounded ever cease to be: borne away out of our hearing it makes its way to the stars: dispersed or removed it cannot be lost. I too, for truth's sake, may have to be dispersed out of my present self which shuts me from you: but I shall find you some day,—you who made me, you who every day make me! A part of you cut off, I suffer pain because I *am* still part of you. If I had no part in you I should suffer nothing. But I do, I do. One is told how, when a man has lost a limb, he still feels it,—not the pleasure of it but the pain. Dearest, are you aware of me now?

Because I am suffering, you shall not think I am entirely miserable. But here and now I am all unfinished ends. Desperately I need faith at times to tell me that each shoot of pain has a point at which it assuages itself and becomes healing: that pain is not endurance wasted; but that I and my weary body have a goal which will give a meaning to all this, somehow, somewhere: never, I begin to fear, here, while this body has charge of me.

Dearest, I lay my heart down on yours and cry: and having worn myself out with it and ended, I kiss your lips and bless God that I have known you.

I have not said—I never could say it—" Let the day perish wherein Love was born!" I forget nothing of you: you are clear to me,—all but one thing: why we have become as we are now, one whole, parted and sent different ways. And yet so near! On my most sleepless nights my pillow is yours: I wet your face with my tears and cry, " Sleep well."

To-night also, Beloved, sleep well! Night and morning I make you my prayer.

## LETTER LXXVII.

My own one beloved, my dearest dear! Want me, please want me! I will keep alive for you. Say you wish me to live,—not come to you: don't say that if you can't—but just wish me to live, and I will. Yes, I will do anything, even live, if you tell me to do it. I will be stronger than all the world or fate, if you have any wish about me at all. Wish well, dearest, and surely the knowledge will come to me. Wish big things of me, or little things: wish me to sleep, and I will sleep better because of it. Wish anything of me: only not that I should love you better. I can't, dearest, I can't. Any more of that, and love would go out of my body and leave it clay. If you would even wish *that*, I would be happy at finding a way to do your will below ground more perfectly than any I found on it. Wish, wish: only wish something for me to do. Oh, I could rest if I had but your little finger to love. The tyranny of love is when it makes no bidding at all. That you have no want

or wish left in you as regards me is my continual
despair.   My own, my beloved, my tormentor
and comforter, my ever dearest dear, whom I
love so much!

## LETTER LXXVIII.

To-night, Beloved, the burden of things is
too much for me. Come to me somehow, dear
ghost of all my happiness, and take me in your
arms! I ache and ache, not to belong to you.
I do: I must. It is only our senses that divide
us; and mine are all famished servants waiting
for their master. They have nothing to do but
watch for you, and pretend that they believe you
will come. Oh, it is grievous!

Beloved, in the darkness do you feel my kisses?
They go out of me in sharp stabs of pain: they
must go *somewhere* for me to be delivered of
them only with so much suffering. Oh, how
this should make me hate you, if that were possible: how, instead, I love you more and more,
and shall, dearest, and will till I die!

I *will* die, because in no other way can I express how much I love you. I am possessed by
all the despairing words about lost happiness that
the poets have written. They go through me
like ghosts: I am haunted by them: but they are

bloodless things. It seems when I listen to all
the other desolate voices that have ever cried,
that I alone have blood in me. Nobody ever
loved as I love since the world began.

There, dearest, take this, all this bitter wine
of me poured out until I feel in myself only the
dregs left: and still in them is the fire and the
suffering.

No: but I will be better: it is better to have
known you than not. Give me time, dearest, to
get you to heart again! I cannot leave you like
this: not with such words as these for " good-
night! "

Oh, dear face, dear unforgetable lost face, my
soul strains up to look for you through the blind
eyes that have been left to torment me because
they can never behold you. Very often I have
seen you looking grieved, shutting away some
sorrow in yourself quietly: but never once angry
or impatient at any of the small follies of men.
Come, then, and look at me patiently now! I
am your blind girl: I must cry out because I
cannot see you. Only make me believe that you
yet think of me as, when you so unbelievably
separated us, you said you had always found me
—" the dearest and most true-hearted woman a
man could pray to meet." Beloved, if in your
heart I am still that, separation does not matter.
I can wait, I can wait.

I kiss your feet: even to-morrow may bring the light. God bless you! I pray it more than ever; because to me to-night has been so very dark.

## LETTER LXXIX.

DEAREST: I have not written to you for three weeks. At last I am better again. You seem to have been waiting for me here: always wondering when I would come back. I do come back, you see.

Dear heart, how are you? I kiss your feet; you are my one only happiness, my great one. Words are too cold and cruel to write anything for me. Picture me: I am too weak to write more, but I have written this, and am so much better for it.

Reward me some day by reading what is here. I kiss, because of you, this paper which I am too tired to fill any more.

Love, nothing but love! Into every one of these dead words my heart has been beating, trying to lay down its life and reach to you.

## LETTER LXXX.

A SECRET, dearest, that will be no secret soon:
before I am done with twenty-three I shall have
passed my age.   Beloved, it hurts me more than
I can say that the news of it should come to you
from anyone but me: for this, though I write it,
is already a dead letter, lost like a predestined
soul even in the pains that gave it birth.   Yes,
it does pain me, frightens me even, that I must
die all by myself, and feeling still so young.   I
thought I should look forward to it, but I do not;
no, no, I would give much to put it off for a time,
until I could know what it will mean for me as
regards you.   Oh, if you only knew and *cared,*
what wild comfort I might have in the knowledge!   It seems strange that if I were going
away from the chance of a perfect life with you
I should feel it with less pain than I feel this.
The dust and the ashes of life are all that I have
to let fall: and it is bitterness itself to part with
them.

How we grow to love sorrow!   Joy is never
so much a possession—it goes over us, incloses
us like air or sunlight; but sorrow goes into us

and becomes part of our flesh and bone. So that I, holding up my hand to the sunshine, see sorrow red and transparent like stained glass between me and the light of day, sorrow that has become inseparably mine, and is the very life I am wishing to keep!

Dearest, will the world be more bearable to you when I am out of it? It is selfish of me not to wish so, since I can satisfy you in this so soon! Every day I will try to make it my wish: or wish that it may be so when the event comes—not a day before. Till then let it be more bearable that I am still alive: grant me, dearest, that one little grace while I live!

Bearable! My sorrow *is* bearable, I suppose, because I do bear it from day to day: otherwise I would declare it not to be. Don't suffer as I do, dearest, unless that will comfort you.

One thing is strange, but I feel quite certain of it: when I heard that I carried death about in me, scarcely an arm's-length away, I thought quickly to myself that it was not the solution of the mystery. Others might have thought that it was: that because I was to die so soon, therefore I was not fit to be your wife. But I know it was not that. I know that whatever hopes death in me put an end to, you would have married me and loved me patiently till I released you, as I am to so soon.

It is always this same woe that crops up: nothing I can ever think can account for what has been decreed.  That too is a secret: mine comes to meet it.  When it arrives shall I know?

And not a word, not a word of this can reach you ever!  Its uses are wrung out and drained dry to comfort me in my eternal solitude.

Good-night; very soon it will have to be good-by.

## LETTER LXXXI.

BELOVED: I woke last night and believed I had your arms round me, and that all storms had gone over me forever. The peace of your love had inclosed me so tremendously that when I was fully awake I began to think that what I held was you dead, and that our reconciliation had come at that great cost.

Something remains real of it all, even now under the full light of day: yet I know you are not dead. Only it leaves me with a hope that at the lesser cost of my own death, when it comes, happiness may break in, and that whichever of us has been the most in poor and needy ignorance will know the truth at last—the truth which is an inseparable need for all hearts that love rightly.

Even now to me the thought of you is a peace passing *all* understanding. Beloved, Beloved, Beloved, all the greetings I ever gave you gather here, and are hungry to belong to you by a better way than I have ever dreamed. I am yours till something more than death swallows me up.

## LETTER LXXXII.

DEAREST: If you will believe any word of mine, you must not believe that I have died of a broken heart should science and the doctors bring about a fulfillment of their present prophesyings concerning me.

I think my heart has held me up for a long time, not letting me know that I was ill: I did not notice. And now my body snaps on a stem that has grown too thin to hold up its weight. I am at the end of twenty-two years: they have been too many for me, and the last has seemed a useless waste of time. It is difficult not to believe that great happiness might have carried me over many more years and built up for me in the end a renewed youth: I asked that quite frankly, wishing to know, and was told not to think it.

So, dearest, whatever comes, whatever I may have written to fill up my worst loneliness, be sure, if you care to be, that though my life was wholly yours, my death was my own, and comes at its right natural time. Pity me, but invent no blame to yourself. My heart has sung of you

even in the darkest days; in the face of everything, the blankness of everything, I mean, it has
clung to an unreasoning belief that in spite of
appearances all had some well in it, above all to
a conviction that—perhaps without knowing it
—you still love me. Believing *that*, it could not
break, could not, dearest. Any other part of
me, but not that.

Beloved, I kiss your face, I kiss your lips and
eyes: my mind melts into kisses when I think of
you. However weak the rest of me grows, my
love shall remain strong and certain. If I could
look at you again, how in a moment you would
fill up the past and the future and turn even my
grief into gold! Even my senses then would forget that they had ever been starved. Dear
" share of the world," you have been out of sight,
but I have never let you go! Ah, if only
the whole of me, the double doubting part of
me as well, could only be so certain as to be able
to give wings to this and let it fly to you! Wish
for it, and I think the knowledge will come to
me!

Good-night! God brings you to me in my
first dream: but the longing so keeps me awake
that sometimes I am a whole night sleepless.

## LETTER LXXXIII.

I AM frightened, dearest, I am frightened at death. Not only for fear it should take me altogether away from you instead of to you, but for other reasons besides,—instincts which I thought gone but am not rid of even yet. No healthy body, or body with power of enjoyment in it, wishes to die, I think: and no heart with any desire still living out of the past. We know nothing at all really: we only think we believe, and hope we know; and how thin that sort of conviction gets when in our extremity we come face to face with the one immovable fact of our own death waiting for us! That is what I have to go through. Yet even the fear is a relief: I come upon something that I can meet at last; a challenge to my courage whether it is still to be found here in this body I have worn so weak with useless lamentations. If I had your hand, or even a word from you, I think I should not be afraid: but perhaps I should. It is all one. Good-by: I am beginning at last to feel a meaning in that word which I wrote at your bidding so long ago. Oh, Beloved, from face to feet, good-by! God be with you wherever you go and I do not!

## LETTER LXXXIV.

DEAREST: I am to have news of you.  Arthur came to me last night, and told me that, if I wished, he would bring me word of you.  He goes to-morrow.  He put out the light that I might not see his face: I felt what was there.

You should know this of him: he has been the dearest possible of human beings to me since I lost you.  I am almost not unblessed when I have him to speak to.  Yet we can say so little together.  I guess all he means.  An endless wish to give me comfort:—and I stay selfish. The knowledge that he would stolidly die to serve me hardly touches me.

Oh, look kindly in his eyes if you see him: mine will be looking at you out of his!

## LETTER LXXXV.

GOOD-MORNING, Beloved; there is sun shining. I wonder if Arthur is with you yet?

If faith could still remove mountains, surely
I should have seen you long ago. But if I were
to see you now, I should fear that it meant you
were dead.

That the same world should hold you and me
living and unseen by each other is a great mystery. Will love ever explain it?

I wish I could bid the sun stand still over your
meeting with Arthur so that I might know. We
were so like each other once. Time has worn
it off: but he is like what I was. Will you remember me well enough to recognize me in him,
and to be a little pitiful to my weak longing for
a word this one last time of all? Beloved, I
press my lips to yours, and pray—speak!

## LETTER LXXXVI.

DEAREST: To-day Arthur came and brought me your message: I have at my heart your " profoundly grateful remembrances." Somewhere else unanswered lies your prayer for God to bless me. To answer that, dearest, is not in His hands but in yours. And the form of your message tells me it will not be,—not for this body and spirit that have been bound together so long in truth to you.

I set down for you here—if you should ever, for love's sake, send and make claim for any message back from me—a profoundly grateful remembrance; and so much more, so much more that has never failed.

Most dear, most beloved, you were to me and are. Now I can no longer hold together: but it is my body, not my love that has failed.